"*Pity* is not the word I think of when I think of you."

"Oh? Good." Maddie ate another bite of the dessert, then curiosity about Hagan's comment got the better of her. "What word do you think of?"

"I think of words like *grace. Determination. Courage.*"

"I wasn't very brave up there on the slope."

His eyes met hers, so blue and clear. Eyes that held no false flattery or flirtation. "There are different kinds of courage," he said. "And there are ways in which every one of us is a coward."

She didn't believe Hagan had ever been a coward; he was only saying that to make her feel better. But the knowledge warmed her. She smiled. "Thanks," she said. "You're not such a bad guy after all. Even if you are a player."

"Think what you will about my relationships with women," he said. "You are better off as my friend than you would be as my lover."

The sudden tightness in her chest at his words caught her off guard. Of course she didn't want Hagan as her lover. He was the last man she'd ever consider.

But she couldn't quite ignore the small voice in the back of her head that whispered, *Liar.*

Dear Reader,

One of the things I love almost as much as writing is skiing. But only in my dreams am I as good as Maddie, Hagan and some of the others in this book. Which is one more wonderful thing about telling stories for a living—in my imagination I get to create characters who do things I'd love to do, but never could.

In *The Right Mr. Wrong* I'm returning to my beloved Crested Butte, Colorado, and my cast of imaginary people. After finishing my first Crested Butte story for Harlequin American Romance, *Marriage on Her Mind*, I knew I had to give sexy, enigmatic Hagan his own story. I'd wanted to write about a heroine who had spent her life focusing on a dream, only to lose it. Maddie Alexander may have lost out on her chance of going to the Olympics, but she's far from given up on life. Her striving to start over and find a new dream strikes a chord with Hagan, who is definitely not the shallow playboy he sometimes seems.

I hope you enjoy this book. Please let me know what you think. I love to hear from readers. You can visit me on the Web at www.CindiMyers.com or write to me at Cindi@CindiMyers.com or P.O. Box 991, Bailey, CO 80421.

Best,

Cindi Myers

The Right Mr. Wrong
CINDI MYERS

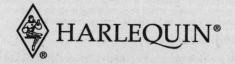

HARLEQUIN®

TORONTO • NEW YORK • LONDON
AMSTERDAM • PARIS • SYDNEY • HAMBURG
STOCKHOLM • ATHENS • TOKYO • MILAN • MADRID
PRAGUE • WARSAW • BUDAPEST • AUCKLAND

ISBN-13: 978-0-373-75203-4
ISBN-10:   0-373-75203-2

THE RIGHT MR. WRONG

Printed in U.S.A.

ABOUT THE AUTHOR

When Cindi Myers is not writing, she loves spending time out of doors. An avid downhill skier, she enjoys hiking and camping in the summer. She lives in the mountains southwest of Denver with her husband and two dogs, all of whom accompany her on most of her outdoor adventures.

Books by Cindi Myers

HARLEQUIN AMERICAN ROMANCE
1182—MARRIAGE ON HER MIND

HARLEQUIN NEXT
MY BACKWARDS LIFE
THE BIRDMAN'S DAUGHTER

HARLEQUIN SIGNATURE SELECT
LEARNING CURVES
BOOTCAMP
  "Flirting with an Old Flame"

HARLEQUIN ANTHOLOGY
A WEDDING IN PARIS
  "Picture Perfect"

Don't miss any of our special offers. Write to us at the following address for information on our newest releases.

Harlequin Reader Service
U.S.: 3010 Walden Ave., P.O. Box 1325, Buffalo, NY 14269
Canadian: P.O. Box 609, Fort Erie, Ont. L2A 5X3

For the people of Crested Butte Mountain Resort.
Thank you.

Chapter One

Love and skiing don't mix. Maddie Alexander recalled this advice, given to her once by an older, cynical colleague, as she stood outside a ski patroller's shack at Crested Butte Mountain Resort and watched an accident in the making. A blonde in a pink jacket was trying to get the attention of a dark-haired guy on twin-tip skis. The sunny day and mild-for-January temperatures had brought out the crowds, including lots of students from nearby Western State College who were still on their winter break. They congregated at the tops of the lifts, checking each other out, enjoying the bright Colorado sun and plentiful snow.

The blonde was so busy eyeing the hunky guy across the slope she neglected to pay attention to where she was skiing. She veered into the mogul field off balance, flailed wildly, caught air as she sailed over a steep bump, and came down in an ungainly heap, while the object of her affections skied on ahead, oblivious.

Memories of other accidents she'd witnessed running through her head, Maddie felt her heart race. The worst situations could start so simply; one minute everything was fine, the next the whole world was full of pain and regret. She clicked into her skis and sped down to the woman, who was lying on her back, moaning. "Are you okay?" Maddie asked.

"My knee." The blonde tried to sit up, then flopped back, anguish contorting her pretty features. "I think I tore up my knee." She uttered a few choice curses, then reverted to moaning.

The blonde's leg was twisted beneath her. Maddie clicked out of her skis and planted them in an X shape on the slope slightly above them. She keyed the mike of her radio and said, "I'm going to need a toboggan over here on Resurrection," identifying the black diamond run where they were located. "I've got a female with a knee injury."

"Hagan's on his way," the voice of Scott Adamson, a fellow patroller, replied.

Maddie frowned. Of course she would draw the one fellow patroller who most rubbed her the wrong way. Not that Hagan Ansdar wasn't an experienced patroller with excellent skills. But he was also one of those men who was just a little too sure of himself—especially when it came to the opposite sex. The kind of man she'd learned the hard way to avoid.

She knelt beside the blonde. "Can you move your right leg at all?"

The woman shook her head, refusing to even attempt a move.

"How about the left leg?" Maddie asked. That leg appeared uninjured, but it was difficult to tell with the camouflage of bulky ski pants.

The blonde shook her head. "I don't want to move

anything in case it hurts," she said. Her face crumpled and tears began to flow. "I can't believe this. This is going to ruin my vacation."

The woman was working herself up to real hysterics. Maddie stifled a groan. When she'd once promised God she'd do anything as long as she could ski again, this wasn't what she'd had in mind. She couldn't believe that she, one of the top ski racers in the world, was now reduced to coddling tourists like this one. She debated the merits of gentle distraction against the expediency of trying to slap some sense into the silly woman. But before she could decide, the woman's crying ceased. She opened her eyes wide and her cheeks flushed pink. "Oh, my," she breathed.

Maddie turned to see a tall figure towing an orange plastic rescue sled skiing toward them. Despite her determination to remain immune to his charms, her essential female nature betrayed her with an inner flutter at the sight of Hagan Ansdar—six feet four, broad shouldered, narrow hipped and blond haired. He might have been a Viking charging to the rescue.

He skidded to a stop a little above them in a spray of snow. Maddie stood and walked up to meet him. "What is the trouble here?" he asked, his Norwegian accent more pronounced than usual.

"I'm guessing a torn meniscus or ACL," Maddie said.

Hagan raised one eyebrow. "They didn't tell me you have a medical degree."

She flushed. This was exactly the kind of ribbing other patrollers routinely dished out, but coming from Hagan, it rankled. "I don't. But I've seen enough of these injuries to recognize a classic." She might be the newest member of Crested Butte ski patrol, but ten years on the World Cup circuit had given her a front-row seat to some truly spectacular crashes. Not to mention she'd suffered an ACL tear herself five years ago. Her knee throbbed now at the memory. "And I saw her fall."

Hagan frowned and clicked out of his skis. "What is her name?"

"I—I don't know. I haven't asked her yet." She'd been about to when he'd arrived and interrupted her.

He knelt beside the blonde and took her hand. "Hello," he said in a voice that would have melted butter. "I am Hagan. What is your name?"

The blonde's eyes widened at the sight of the Norse god looming over her. "Hi." She flashed a smile of her own. "I'm Julie."

"Well, Julie, is it your knee that hurts?"

"Yeah. My right knee." She raised her head and stared down at her bent leg.

"Does anything else hurt?" Hagan was feeling his way down her leg, his gloved hands moving slowly, making a thorough examination.

He wasn't really feeling her up, Maddie reminded herself, though to a casual observer it might seem that he was being a little *too* thorough.

Julie obviously had no objections, though. She fluttered her lashes at him and spoke breathily. "Just the knee, I think. Though I'm feeling a little light-headed."

"You took quite a fall." Hagan cradled the back of Julie's head and took her hand once more to check her pulse. "You knocked the breath out of yourself."

Julie nodded, her attention fixed on him. Maddie might as well have not existed. She shook her head and began readying the toboggan for transport.

"What happened?" Hagan asked. "How did you fall?"

"I don't know. I was skiing along and all of a sudden, I fell."

Maddie suppressed a snort, but she didn't quite succeed. Hagan gave her a sharp look. "Radio the clinic we are bringing in a young woman with a possible injury to her right knee," he said.

Maddie did as he asked, while he finished examining Julie. Then she maneuvered the sled into position and together they transferred their patient into it. Hagan secured her inside, tucking the blankets around her. "There, you are all comfy now," he said.

Julie beamed up at him. "Yes. Thank you."

Gag me, Maddie thought.

Just then, Scott and another patroller, Eric, arrived with the snowmobile to tow the sled across the mountain to the clinic in the main village. "I'll take her down and get her checked in," Eric volunteered. "I have to be down at the base in a few minutes anyway."

Maddie helped stow Julie's skis in the back, then Eric and Scott set out, Eric pulling the sled while Scott towed him with the snowmobile. Maddie and Hagan would follow on skis to handle the paperwork.

"She will be all right," Hagan said as he watched the snowmobile pull away.

"I'm sure she will." And she'd no doubt be telling all her friends about the "amazing" ski patroller who had "rescued" her. And she wouldn't be talking about Maddie. She glanced at Hagan. "Is it my imagination, or does your accent get thicker whenever you talk to a pretty woman?"

He turned and swept her with a slow, head-to-toe gaze. The look wasn't exactly insulting—more as if he was assessing her. She stiffened, prepared for some comment about her own appearance. She knew she wasn't ugly, but she wasn't a glamour girl like Julie, either. Her years as a pro had stressed practicality over prettiness. Today she wore no makeup and her brown hair was pulled back in a single braid that trailed down between her shoulder blades.

But no insult came her way. Instead, the corners of his mouth turned up in what might have been a smile, which only made him more handsome. "Must be your imagination," he said.

The comment threw her off balance emotionally, the way everything about the man seemed to do. Her first day on patrol no less than three other women on the team had made reference to Hagan as the local Don Juan. They'd said this with the affection one might use to refer to a bratty younger brother, as if it was merely part of his charm. They'd further explained he exclusively pursued tourists and other temporary visitors to the area, therefore she had nothing to worry about from him—the implication being she had no chance of winning him for herself.

As if she wanted him. She knew all about handsome playboys. She'd once dated a slalom racer known as the Italian Stallion, and her first season as a pro skier she'd had her heart broken by an Austrian who later bragged to *Sports Illustrated* that he'd slept with every female racer on the U.S. Olympic Team.

It was bad enough she was working as a ski patroller; she didn't need to put up with any hassle from a player like Hagan.

They hiked up the slope to where their skis were planted in the snow. "What were you snickering about when I asked her how the accident happened?" Hagan asked as they clicked boots into bindings once more.

"She told you she didn't know how the accident happened, but the truth is, she was ogling some guy and not paying attention to where she was going."

"I thought men were the only ones who ogled." He sounded amused by the idea.

"Ha!" As if he wasn't perfectly aware of the women who stared after him wherever he went.

They skied to the bottom of the East River lift. They'd ride back up and from there head to the front side of the mountain and the main village clinic. Hagan pulled out in front of her and Maddie took this as a challenge. He might have longer legs, but she was willing to bet no one on the patrol team was faster than her.

Sure enough, she soon overtook him. There was nothing like the feeling of flying over the snow, the white noise of rushing wind in her ears and the sensation of being suspended in time. She wove effortlessly around slower skiers and arrived well ahead of Hagan at the lift line.

She grinned at his approach, ready to tease him for his slowness, but he silenced her with a stern look and sterner words. "You think you are still racing?" he asked, as he slid beside her in line.

She couldn't think of an answer that wouldn't be an admission that she'd been trying to stay ahead of him, so she remained silent and looked over her shoulder for the approaching chair.

He waited until they were on the chair and headed up the slope before he spoke. "We pull people's passes for skiing that fast," he said. "You are no longer a ski racer."

The reprimand galled. As if she needed a refresher course in ski safety from this two-bit Don Juan. "I don't need you to remind me I'm no longer a racer," she snapped. "It's not something I'm likely to forget." Every morning when she awoke the reality hit her anew; the one thing she had wanted most in life was out of her reach forever, stolen by one miscalculated move on an icy slope in Switzerland.

"I am only reminding you to slow down. That is all." His voice was surprisingly gentle.

She ducked her head. His calmness was even more annoying than the reprimand. But she was woman enough to admit she was wrong. She *wasn't* on a race course and she probably should slow down. Much as she hated to. "I'll be more careful in the future," she said stiffly.

Not for the first time, she'd let her impulsiveness make her lose her focus and forget her purpose. She would have thought by now she'd be over that, but maybe there were some lessons a person never learned.

HAGAN STUDIED the woman next to him as she stared straight ahead. He considered himself an expert on the ever-changing nature of women, but Maddie Alexander was more mercurial than most. In the space of a few minutes she'd gone from teasing to defiant to contrite.

As the newest member of the patrol, she had endured the good-natured harassment of her fellow team members with grace, but something he had said—or maybe the very fact of his presence—had set her off.

"What is it about me—exactly—that you do not like?" he asked when they reached the top of the lift.

She whirled to face him, almost falling as she did so. She managed to recover her balance and ski away from the top of the lift before she stopped and turned to him again with what passed for composure. "Don't be ridiculous. I don't know you well enough to dislike you."

"Then maybe you should get to know me better."

It was a glib line, one he had used before, but as soon as it rolled off his tongue he knew it was the wrong approach to take with her. She glared at him, then planted her pole and skied away.

He watched her go, admiring the curve of her hips and her expert form as she skied down a small hill and across an open flat. He would bet she was beautiful on a race course, gliding gracefully around turns, clipping gates with efficient speed.

He shook his head to dispel the image. Maddie was beautiful all right, but she was also a coworker, and a local. Someone he was likely to see every day, therefore off his list as a potential date. He had learned long ago to stick with tourists—they allowed for an enjoyable short-term affair and a quick, neat exit. No complications.

He skied down and joined her as she propped her skis in the rack outside the clinic. He stepped forward and held the door open for her. She glanced up at him and mumbled her thanks, then slipped by, careful not to brush against him.

So much for worrying he might have to watch his step around her to keep her from getting too interested in him. For whatever reason, she wanted nothing to do with him. Not the usual reaction he got from women—and why?

And why was he letting her rejection bother him so much?

They found their patient, Julie, sitting up on an exam table, her injured knee wrapped in towels and ice. Hagan's friend, Dr. Ben Romney, examined her X-rays. "Your turn on the mountain today?" Hagan asked.

"That's right," Ben said. He turned to Julie. "You've got a little tear in your meniscus, but you're going to be fine. I don't even think you'll need surgery."

"Thanks to Hagan." Julie beamed at him. "I'm sure I'd be much worse off if he hadn't arrived so quickly to take care of me."

He smiled automatically. Julie was pretty, with expensive ski clothes and a flirtatious manner. But with her knee banged up she wouldn't be doing much partying for a few weeks. And while he was not opposed to taking advantage of his job to meet women, he shied away from involvement with those who were physically injured on his watch.

Some—Maddie perhaps—would say this was skewed ethics on his part, but he made up his own rules for his life and that was one of them.

Ben left Julie to the care of his nurse and motioned for Hagan and Maddie to follow him into his office. "Looks like you've made another conquest," he said to Hagan after he had shut the office door.

Hagan shook his head. "She will be cutting her vacation short to take care of her injury," he said. He dropped into one of two chairs in front of Ben's desk. "Have you met Maddie? She is our newest patroller."

"Pleased to meet you, Maddie." Ben offered his hand. "Ben Romney."

"It's good to meet you, Dr. Romney."

"Ben, please. What brings you to ski patrol?"

"I thought it was time to try something different," she said. "Ski patrol sounded interesting."

The explanation struck Hagan as incomplete. Why would a world-class athlete retreat to a somewhat remote Colorado resort when she might have scored a lucrative gig as a rep for an equipment manufacturer, an outdoor clothing model or even the resident pro on a resort's marketing payroll? Why put up with the hard work, injured tourists and low pay of ski patrol?

"She was a ski racer," he said. "World Cup. Headed for the Olympics." Apparently she had left the team after a bad accident, but he did not know the details.

Ben leaned forward, definitely more interested now. "What's your last name?"

She sent Hagan a pained look. Hey, why was she ticked at him? It wasn't as if her past was a big secret. "Alexander. Maddie Alexander."

"Awesome Alexander!" Ben grinned. "I remember reading about you in *Sports Illustrated*."

"Yeah." Her gloomy expression was more worthy of a write-up in *Mortician's Monthly*.

"You were written up in some of the medical journals, too," Ben said. "The titanium repair on your tibia? And the artificial joint in your hip?"

She nodded, her face pale. Hagan stood and pushed

a chair toward her. She looked as if she might faint. "Sit down," he ordered, and she did so. He glared at Ben.

Ben had the grace to flush. "Sorry. I forget not everyone's as interested in catastrophic medicine as I am. Heather has to remind me not to discuss surgery at dinner."

"She is a wise woman," Hagan said. Mostly because Heather had finally gotten over the silly crush she had had on him last summer and had focused on a man who really cared for her—the way Hagan never could have.

There was a knock and the nurse stuck her head in the door. "Your patient is ready to go," she said.

"We had better get back to work, too," Hagan said as Maddie popped to her feet.

"It was nice meeting you, Maddie." Ben offered his hand. "Welcome to Crested Butte."

"Thanks." She shook his hand and flashed a warm smile. Hagan felt a pinch of jealousy that such a look had not been directed at him.

Which only proved his ego was as big as the next guy's. He was not interested in dating Maddie, but there was no reason they could not be friends.

They followed Ben into the clinic's reception room, and found Julie balancing on a pair of crutches. "Oh, Hagan? Could you help me out to my friend's car?" She fluttered her eyelashes and smiled at him.

"Of course." He took one crutch and let her lean on him instead as they made their way to an SUV idling out front. He deposited her in the passenger seat and she pressed a slip of paper into his hand. "Call me," she whispered, then kissed his cheek.

He pocketed the paper and stepped back, making no commitment as the SUV pulled away.

"I'll go fill out the report," Maddie said, pushing past him. "You can add your part later."

She grabbed her skis from the rack and headed around the side of the building. Ben came to stand alongside Hagan. "What did you do to her?" he asked.

"Nothing," he said.

Ben looked as if he did not believe this. "You didn't hit on her, did you?" he asked.

Hagan scowled at him. "No, you know I stay away from the locals."

"Yeah." Ben looked again in the direction Maddie had vanished. "Maybe she's jealous of you and Julie baby."

"Not likely." He would know if she were interested in him—she showed none of the usual signs.

"Maybe you should consider breaking your own rule," Ben said. "She's good-looking and you two have skiing and patrol in common."

"Not my type." Yes, Maddie was good-looking and independent and she had an interesting background, but she was too prickly for his tastes. Not to mention that being around her made him feel too edgy and un-comfortable. "I will stick with the tourists." His policy of avoiding emotional entanglements with women had served him well for the past ten years. He saw no need to abandon it now.

Ben shook his head. "If you think that's going to keep you from getting caught one day, you've got another think coming. Just ask Max."

Hagan's best friend Max Overbridge and newcomer Casey Jernigan were engaged to be married in the summer, as soon as the snow melted enough off the

Mountain Garden to hold the wedding there. Hagan was slated to serve as best man. "The difference between me and Max," Hagan said, "is that Max wanted to be caught, no matter what he says different. Me, I know better."

Marriage was a velvet-lined pit, a lure that made a man believe he could find eternal happiness. But there were sharpened sticks waiting at the bottom of the pit. He had been there before and never intended to experience that pain again. Better to indulge in the occasional casual fling with a woman who would soon leave town than to get involved with a woman like Maddie who could truly turn his world upside down.

Chapter Two

Maddie finished up the accident report then left it in Hagan's box for him to sign off on. If he had any questions, he could radio her, but she wouldn't wait around for him. She didn't need him thinking she was an adoring fan begging for his attention. Everyone said he was an excellent patroller—and from what she'd seen so far, she'd have to agree—but his Don Juan act was simply too much. When her life was more in order and she was ready to settle into a relationship again, it would be with a man she could respect and count on—not a player like Hagan.

For now, she'd try to keep her distance from him and not risk saying something that might jeopardize her job.

She was on her way out of the patrol shack when her roommate, fellow patroller Andrea Dawson, hailed her. Andrea was the only woman on patrol who was almost as short as Maddie's own five feet. Her straight black hair and almond eyes revealed her Asian heritage. Originally from China, she'd been adopted as an infant by a local couple and had practically grown up on skis. "You busy?" she asked Maddie.

Maddie shook her head. "No. What's up?"

"We just got a report of a couple of snowboarders ducking ropes over by Spellbound and Phoenix. The area's still closed for avalanche control. I need to go check it out. I could use some backup."

"Sure." Yellow ropes were used to mark the ski area boundaries and to close off areas considered too unstable or dangerous for skiing or riding. But there were always people who thought the rules didn't apply to them, who risked ducking under the ropes.

"I hate this part of the job," Andrea said as she and Maddie rode the Silver Queen lift up the mountain. "These guys always want to give me lip and it's such a hassle. If it weren't for the fact they could trigger an avalanche or get hurt I'd tell them to go ahead and kill themselves."

Maddie laughed. "Nobody likes ragging on other people, but if anybody gets mouthy with me, I let them have it. It's a great way to vent my frustrations—if they deserve it."

"Guess I'll watch and learn from an expert then."

"Maybe we'll be lucky and they'll listen to reason."

"Yeah, like how often does that happen?"

From the top of Silver Queen, they headed into Paradise Bowl and up the North Face lift. They found the two snowboarders in a deep gully a few hundred yards beyond the ropes closing off the popular Spellbound Glades, an area of double-black runs that usually didn't open until the snowpack had built up later in the season.

One of the boarders, wearing a bright green stocking cap, was hung up on a snag, trying to wrench his board free, while his friend, in a camouflage snowboarding suit, stood downslope, shouting at him to hurry.

"Having trouble?" Maddie asked as she and Andrea stopped above the two.

Green cap scowled up at her. "I'm okay," he muttered, and went back to working his board loose.

"You guys are in a closed area," Andrea said.

"We are?" Red Jacket's innocent look might have been practiced in a mirror for just such an occasion. "We thought we might have gotten off the trail, but we weren't sure." He grinned. "Sorry."

"Dude, we saw your tracks where you slid under the ropes," Maddie said. "Right next to a sign that said closed."

"What's the big deal?" Green Hat asked, his board free at last. "We're not hurting anybody."

"Not yet," Andrea said. "But this area is closed for a reason. You could trigger an avalanche."

"Yeah, and then we have to go to all the trouble of digging out your bodies," Maddie said. "We hate that."

"We hate that," Red Jacket mimicked.

Maddie looked at Andrea. "I think these two just lost their passes," she said.

"There's also the fine," Andrea added. "Up to one thousand dollars."

"You have to catch us first," Green Hat said, and took off down the slope.

"Yep, they're getting the fine, too," Maddie said. But as she stared down the rocky, vertical slope, she felt a little queasy.

It wasn't any steeper than anything she'd skied as a racer, but merely looking at it made her palms sweat and her heart race. It was strange how only certain runs and situations—such as this one—brought back the horror of her accident. She'd hoped being on patrol, skiing every day and confronting terrain like this would help her get over her fear, but so far this cure wasn't working.

"We don't have to chase them," Andrea said.

"We don't?" Maddie thought she did a good job of hiding her relief.

Andrea shook her head. "Nah. This funnels down to the top of the East River lift. We'll radio for someone to meet them there." She unclipped her radio from her pack and gave the description of the two boarders, requesting someone hold them at the top of East River. Then she and Maddie shouldered their skis and hiked up out of the closed area.

Maddie wished she had a camera when, twenty minutes later, Red Jacket and Green Hat looked up from their conversation with patrollers Eric and Marcie to see Andrea and Maddie coming toward them.

"Hello, guys." Andrea smiled. "Looks like we caught up with you after all." Before the men could say anything, each patroller had pulled out a pair of scissors and snipped off the boarders' passes. "You can either come with us quietly and fill out the paperwork," Andrea said. "Or we'll call the police and have you arrested."

"Arrested for what?" Green Hat asked.

"Trespassing on private property and violating the Colorado Ski Safety Act, for a start." Maddie glanced at Andrea. "I'm sure we can come up with a few other things if you don't think that's enough."

The two boarders exchanged looks, shoulders slumped, then admitted defeat. They waited quietly while Eric started up a snowmobile to take them off the mountain.

Once the two boarders were taken care of, it was after three-thirty and the lifts were beginning to shut down. Andrea and Maddie joined the other patrollers in sweeping the mountain—skiing each trail to make sure there were no stranded skiers or riders. It was Maddie's favorite time of day, when she skied the mostly deserted runs, alone with her thoughts and the feeling of freedom soaring over the snow always gave her. For that brief period she wasn't a poorly paid, overworked ski patroller, but an elite athlete who still had the potential for greatness.

By the time Maddie dragged into the locker room, it was after five. She was pleasantly tired, and feeling better about the start of her second week as a patroller. It wasn't her dream job, but it was skiing, and that made it worth something. She sat to take off her ski boots and Andrea slid down the bench to rest beside her.

"There's a party at the Eldo tonight," she said. "You going?"

"What is the Eldo?" Maddie asked.

"It's a place downtown, on Elk Avenue. Everybody hangs out there."

Maddie shook her head. "I'm not really in the partying mood."

"Come on," Andrea pleaded. "Are you just going to hang out at the condo by yourself and brood?"

"I'm not going to brood." But if Maddie were completely honest, that was probably exactly what she'd do.

"You need to get out and meet people," Andrea said. "And there are a lot of good-looking guys in this town. Some of them are even worth knowing."

Guys like Hagan Ansdar? Maddie dismissed the thought. She already knew all she needed to know about Hagan. He was a playboy who took his good looks and athleticism as his due—as if he were somehow immune from mere human frailties that plagued those around him.

"Come on," Andrea said again. "If you don't like it, you can always take the bus back up to the mountain."

Maddie couldn't argue with that reasoning, so ended up seated next to Andrea on the free shuttle bus headed down to the town of Crested Butte, which sat in a little valley a few miles below the ski resort. The main street, Elk Avenue, was lined with restored Victorian buildings and newer buildings made to look old, most painted in bright colors. Light from streetlamps and storefronts spilled across the mounds of snow that lined the sidewalks. Noisy groups of tourists and locals alike navigated the slippery walks and crowded into the restaurants, shops and bars.

The Eldo occupied the second story of a building near the end of the street. The outdoor balcony was already crowded with revelers who greeted newcomers with shouts and whistles. Maddie followed Andrea up the stairs and through the glass-front doors, into the throbbing pulse of music on the jukebox, the crack of pool balls and the low roar of conversation. How many such bars had she been in, all over the globe, with her fellow skiers? This one felt no different, right down to the woman on crutches in the corner, the guy in the knee brace by the bar and the assortment of outlandish knit hats worn by the patrons. This was her world, what she knew. And this feeling of belonging, of recognizing the social landscape, was part of the reason she'd settled for such a menial job as patrolling.

As she and Andrea squeezed past the crowded bar, Maddie waved to a few familiar faces. After only ten days in town she was getting to know people, though more of them recognized her thanks to her brief flirtation with fame. Not for the first time she wished that photographer from *Sports Illustrated* had never snapped the shot of her and two of her teammates posed with their skis and a collection of medals. *America's skiing sweethearts,* the caption had read, and the article inside had described them as the United States's top medal hopes for the 2006 Olympics.

But instead of standing on an Olympic podium, Maddie had watched the games from a hospital bed, alternately weeping and cursing her fate.

She shook off the memory and followed Andrea to a long line of tables pushed together and crowded with Eric, Scott and other patrollers. Hagan was seated a few chairs down from her, with a couple of snowboarders Andrea introduced as Max and Zephyr.

Scott filled plastic cups with beer from a pitcher and passed them to her and Andrea. Maddie didn't really like beer that much, but it was nice to be so readily included in their party. When she'd still been on the circuit, she'd been part of an insular group who'd descend upon a resort en masse. They'd be the ones shoving the tables together and mostly hanging with each other before heading to the next race venue. It had been many years since she'd stayed in one place long enough to really get to know people, and she still wasn't sure how to respond to the friendliness almost everyone in town had shown her. She wanted to return their warmth, of course, but she didn't want to come across as over-eager and needy.

After years as a skiing nomad, she was out of practice making new friends. It didn't help that she had no idea how long she'd stay in Crested Butte. Unable to imagine a winter away from skiing, she'd taken the patroller's job as a stopgap—something to do until she figured out where to go next. Ever since her injury her life had been plagued by uncertainty and the feeling that everything she did was temporary. She was on edge, waiting for some-thing, but she had no idea what that something would be.

Maybe the next thing to do was to go with the flow. Get to know these people. It couldn't hurt, and it might help her to feel less alone. Less isolated by her private misery.

She studied the dreadlocked blonde next to Hagan. "Zephyr?" she repeated, not sure she'd heard the name correctly.

"Yeah. I'm a rock guitarist." He pantomimed play-ing a guitar.

"Cool." Maybe he was famous and she didn't know it. She'd slept, breathed, thought and lived nothing but skiing for the previous ten years, so she was a little behind on pop culture.

"Right now I'm taking a break from music to pursue fame as a snowboarder," Zephyr continued. "I'm enter-ing the Free Skiing competition next month."

The Free Skiing competition was the biggest event in the country, with the serious daredevils of skiing and snowboarding competing. All the big names in alternative winter sports would be there. "Have you ever competed before?" she asked.

"No. I'm not really the competitive kind." Zephyr grinned. "But I'm good."

"He is." The man next to him, a muscular guy named Max, said. "He's also crazy."

"It helps to be crazy to compete." She took a long drink, not really tasting the beer. What else but insanity drove a person to do things like race at top speed down steep, icy mountains or jump off cliffs into canyons of snow? There was no greater adrenaline rush. She wondered if she'd ever stop missing that feeling.

"I think you ought to be committed." A woman who could have been Jennifer Anniston's double frowned at Zephyr, who sat across from her at the table. "Aren't you afraid, doing all those crazy stunts?"

"No. I know I can do it."

"You should be afraid," Maddie said. "In racing we had a saying—it's not *if* you get hurt, it's *when*."

He shrugged. "I refuse to think about it," he said. "It's a Zen thing."

"Zen is drinking a nice cup of tea at my coffee shop and listening to Indian flute music," the woman said. "Zen is not hucking your body off of cliffs on a snowboard."

Zephyr grinned again. "Aww, Trish. It's nice to know you care."

Trish flushed. "I care about stray dogs and lost tourists, too. Don't assume it means anything."

"Some people believe confronting fear makes them stronger." Hagan's softly accented voice cut through the barroom chatter. Maddie looked over to find his gaze on her, intense but unreadable.

"Some people say a lot of things that don't make sense," she said. She leaned toward him, refusing to look away or let him think he could intimidate her. "What about you? What fears do you confront?"

The creases fanning out from the corners of his eyes sharpened, then he looked away. "I did not say facing fears was always a good idea. Sometimes it is better to avoid the situation altogether."

She had expected him to say he wasn't afraid of anything. His answer intrigued her—what did a man like Hagan have to fear? Then she was annoyed with herself. What did she care what Mr. Handsome Hagan thought or did?

She turned and grabbed Scott's arm. "Let's dance."

"Uh…okay." He let her pull him onto the minuscule dance floor and began to move, a little stiffly. "Just so you know, Lisa and I are kind of an item." He nodded toward a curvy redhead who worked in the resort ticket office.

She hadn't realized, and felt a little foolish. "It's only a dance," she said. All she'd really wanted was to get away from the table for a while.

"Right. Just wanted to make sure you knew that."

She'd hoped getting up and moving around would help her feel better and keep her mind out of the downward spiral that thoughts of skiing and her fears could bring on. Instead her knee hurt and a different kind of pain had settled in her stomach. Coming here was a mistake—not only coming to the Eldo tonight, but moving to Crested Butte and joining the ski patrol. She'd picked Crested Butte because it was far from a city, off the racing circuit and offered the opportunity to ski. Skiing was what she knew. What she was good at. But she didn't really belong here, in this town where everyone knew everyone and all got along so well. Traveling, competing and training was the life she knew—nothing else felt right.

As soon as the song ended, she mumbled her thanks to Scott, then grabbed her coat and slipped out the door. The others at the table were focused on Zephyr and his friend Bryan's arm-wrestling match; the loser would have to wax the winner's snowboard.

Maddie hurried down the stairs into night air so cold it felt like breathing ice. She stood on the sidewalk in front of the bar and stared up at a sky studded with stars like silver glitter on black glass. *Get a grip,* she scolded herself. She had a good life. She needed to focus on all the great things ahead instead of what she'd lost.

But what was ahead for her? For the previous decade she'd had a clear goal—to get to the Olympics. To be recognized as one of the top ski racers in the world.

All that was gone now, and she had nothing to replace it. The knowledge made her feel empty and lost.

"If you want to look at stars, there are better places than on the street in front of the Eldo." Hagan came to stand beside her. He was wearing a red and black parka, but his head was bare, the night breeze ruffling his white-blond hair.

"You're going to freeze without a hat," she said.

He shoved his hands in his jacket pockets. "Where I grew up, it is colder than this."

She went back to looking at the stars. It was either that or keep staring at him. Whether it was his good looks, or the quiet strength that radiated from him, or the solid confidence she envied, being with Hagan made her hyperaware of every one of her own flaws.

"Are you all right?" he asked after a moment.

"I'm fine." Freezing, but fine. She hugged her parka closer around her body. "I'm going to catch a bus back up to the mountain and turn in early."

This was his cue to go back into the bar, but he fell in step beside her as she began walking toward the bus stop. She glared at him. "Why did you follow me out here?"

"You interest me."

The idea made her catch her breath. She'd heard all about Hagan's rule about not dating locals. "Why? You have a thing for washed-up athletes?"

He raised one eyebrow. "Do you have something against Norsemen? Or men in general? Why are you so prickly?"

Her shoulders sagged. He was right. She was being a witch with a capital *B,* taking her bad mood out on him. Yes, he was a player and his confidence—which bordered on arrogance—annoyed her. But so far he hadn't made any moves on her or done anything to warrant her hostility. And he was her coworker on patrol, someone she'd be seeing a lot of in the coming weeks and months. She needed to learn to get along with him. "I'm sorry," she said. "Why don't we start over?" At the bus stop in front of the Chamber of Commerce, she stopped and offered him her hand. "Hi, I'm Maddie Alexander. I'm new here."

A hint of a smile formed on his lips. "A pleasure to meet you, Ms. Alexander. I am Hagan Ansdar." He took her hand in his and fixed her with his clear blue eyes. His clasp was firm, his gaze steady, and his soft accent made every word smooth and exotic. No wonder he had women falling at his feet. She pulled her hand away before she melted right there in the snow, shocked by her reaction. So much for thinking her cynicism about men like Hagan made her immune to his charms.

"What brings you to Crested Butte, Ms. Alexander?" he asked, continuing the charade that they had just met.

"It's beautiful country. And I thought ski patrol would be interesting."

"I would have thought after your career as a racer ended you would have had your choice of jobs," he said. "Representing a ski equipment or clothing manufacturer, or skiing as the pro at a high-profile resort."

"Those jobs go to the medal winners."

"But ski patrol—" he glanced at her "—it doesn't pay much."

No, but she'd made some money in her racing career and managed to save a portion of it. What she'd needed more than money was a place to lay low and figure out what to do with the rest of her life.

"I really appreciated the patrollers who helped me when I was injured," she said. "The doctors and nurses, too, but I don't have a medical degree and I wanted a job that would allow me to ski every day. I may not be able to race anymore, but I still love skiing."

"You are a beautiful skier. You have a natural grace."

She didn't know which unnerved her more—the unexpected compliment or the knowledge that he'd been watching her.

She changed the subject. "How did a man from Norway end up in Crested Butte, Colorado?" she asked.

When he didn't answer right away, she glanced at him again. His mouth was compressed into a thin line, his brow furrowed in thought. "I think for many people Crested Butte is a good place to escape. To hide out, even."

The words sent a sudden shiver up her spine. Was he accusing her of running away? Or was he answering her question in an oblique way?

The bus arrived, filled with rowdy tourists. She and Hagan were forced to take seats at opposite ends of the vehicle. But from her position at the back of the bus, she studied his profile and wondered if she'd been wrong to dismiss him as merely a player.

HAGAN STARED STRAIGHT ahead as the bus made its way up the mountain road to the resort. He was glad the crowd had separated him from Maddie. He needed the distance. Standing in the cold with her just now, watching the play of emotion on her face, he had been surprised by how much he wanted to kiss her.

He had kissed a lot of women in the past few years, slept with almost as many. The experiences had been pleasurable pastimes, things he had wanted to do. But never had he felt the *need* to reach out to someone that he felt with Maddie.

The idea disturbed him. He was not a man who needed other people. He enjoyed being with friends, and he liked the women he dated, but he didn't depend on them to make him happy. Investing too much of oneself in another person was a sure road to disappointment.

He got off the bus at the first stop and walked past rows of condos to the parking lot where he kept his truck. From there it was another five miles up winding roads to his cabin on forest service land. It was a rustic two-room affair originally designed as a summer retreat, but he had added a woodstove and insulation, a king-size bed and new appliances, turning it into comfortable bachelor quarters.

He shoved open the door he seldom bothered to lock and was greeted by a fat gray striped tomcat, who wove around his ankles and demanded supper in a loud voice. "Hush," Hagan said with no malice in his voice. The cat, dubbed Fafner after a dragon in Norse legend, had showed up two years ago and refused to leave.

Hagan opened a can of the gourmet food the feline preferred, then turned on the computer that sat on a fold-down desk in one corner of the main room. A galley kitchen and a loft bedroom and bath completed the living quarters. He added wood to the stove and shed his coat, then poured a beer, made a plate of cheese, sausage and crackers and carried them to the desk.

Moments later, he was engrossed in the software program he had been tinkering with. Occupying his free time with software design was a holdover from his previous life. But where once it had been his passion, now it was merely a hobby no one knew about. A thing he did only for himself.

When he was satisfied he could do no more with the program for now, he sat back and sipped the beer and studied the cabin. Over the door was a pair of old-fashioned wooden skis, the kind they had still used when he was a boy, skiing to school in Fredrikstad. On a shelf by the stove was a Norwegian ceramic stein his sister had sent him two Christmases ago.

He liked this place. It was his alone, a sanctuary where his friends seldom visited and he never brought women. It was orderly and comfortable, like his life. He had work he enjoyed, and though he was not prosperous financially, he had savings put away. He had good friends in town and never had to sleep alone unless he wanted to. He was satisfied.

But lately he had been restless. When Maddie had left the Eldo this evening, he had been ready to depart himself. He had decided to call the number on the slip of paper Julie had handed him that afternoon to see how she was doing. Maybe offer to stop by her place and bring a bottle of wine.

Instead he had found himself distracted by this newcomer to town, this graceful, intense young woman who fairly burned with some unnamed anger and passion. He was drawn to her, curious and more than a little wary.

Something about Maddie Alexander affected him in a way no woman had in a long time. He did not necessarily like it, but he wanted to understand it. If he could figure out why she made him feel this way, he would know better how to handle it—and better how to avoid allowing this fascination with her to turn into something more.

Chapter Three

Maddie woke the next morning to temperatures near zero and snow coming down hard. The kind of conditions when races would have been canceled and she would have been able to stay in bed and sleep the day away. But ski patrollers didn't have that luxury, and she was on duty this morning. As she padded about the kitchen making coffee, she looked with envy at Andrea's closed door. Her roommate was off today. Too bad the two of them couldn't trade places.

At least she wasn't on the avalanche control team. Those guys were on the mountain at dawn, setting off charges to loosen unstable deposits of snow. Of course, they were all adrenaline junkies who relished the opportunity to legally play with explosives. Testosterone in action.

At the patrol shack near the top of the Silver Queen lift, she checked the duty roster. "Shouldn't be much happening today," Scott said, coming up behind her. "It's a weekday, and the weather is keeping in everyone but the hard-core skiers, boarders and vacationers determined to get every last dollar's worth from their passes.

Main thing is to watch for people getting in over their heads."

"We should have good skiing with all this fresh powder."

At the sound of the familiar accent, she turned and saw Hagan filling the doorway of the shack. "I am heading over to Peel." He nodded to Maddie. "Will you come with me?"

Peel was a lift-served run in the extreme terrain on the front side of the resort. She'd toured the area during her orientation, but had avoided it after that. "That's okay," she said. "Find someone else."

"I do not want to go with anyone else," he said. His blue eyes offered a silent challenge. "Is it the terrain you do not like—or me?"

After their conversation last night, she could no longer claim to dislike the man. He unsettled her, intrigued her and sometimes surprised her, but she also trusted his skill as a patroller. He was one of the senior members of the team, a man others called upon in the toughest situations. If she was going to venture onto extreme runs, he was the person to do it with. And hadn't he said last night people could overcome their fears by facing them? It was one of the things she'd joined patrol to do. And it wasn't as if she hadn't skied worse in her years on the racing circuit.

"All right," she said. "I'll go with you."

"Be careful," Scott said. "It's really nasty out there."

Wind-driven snow hit them like needles when they stepped out of the patrol shack. Maddie ducked her head and zipped her parka to her chin. Any sane person would be sitting in front of a fire with a cup of hot cocoa now instead of outside on a pair of skis.

"It will be better when we get down in the trees," Hagan called over the howling wind.

She nodded and followed him down a narrow run between the trees. As promised the wind was blocked here. The heavy dump of snow had buried all the rocks and snags visible the day before and transformed the run into a gentle roller coaster. Maddie relaxed. This wasn't so bad after all. And they had the run all to themselves.

But as soon as they left the shelter of the trees, they hit whiteout conditions again. Sky merged with ground and it was difficult to tell up from down. Maddie slowed, and fought stomach-churning vertigo. She reminded herself of all the techniques for overcoming this phenomena—bend her knees more, ski close to the trees, focus on landmarks—in this case the back of Hagan's red patrol jacket barely visible ahead in the swirling snow.

They skied over to the high lift and grabbed hold of the T-bar. They were alone up here today, with the exception of the bored attendant in the lift shack. The normally busy runs were deserted; they might have been the only skiers on the mountain. Ordinarily she'd love the solitude and the chance to fly through the powder. But right now her muscles were rigid with the effort to keep her thoughts focused and not spiral to images of every crash she'd ever witnessed…or experienced.

Maddie tightened her hold on the T-bar and ducked her head against the wind-driven blasts of snow. At the top, she slid next to Hagan. "Only a crazy person would ski in this," she said.

Hagan nodded. "Some people think only a crazy person would race on skis," he added.

Right. Maybe she had been a little crazy in those days. She stared out at the swirling snow that obscured the view of the resort and town below. Days like this on the racing circuit almost always meant bad news.

"Is Peel all right, or do you want to hike to Peak or Banana Funnel?" He named two other double black diamond runs.

She shook her head. "No hiking. The weather's too brutal."

She looked down the slope, trying to scope out the run, but everything about the place looked different from her visit during her orientation two weeks ago. Then, the best path down had been clearly visible, the tracks of other skiers etched between rocks and trees. Now everything was obscured.

"Then let us go," Hagan said. Without waiting for an answer, he set off down the run. He disappeared in the swirling whiteness and Maddie followed him. But she had barely negotiated her first turn when she froze, and stared down the steep slope, heart pounding.

"You can do this," she whispered, and gripped her poles with more strength. But there was no conviction in her voice. Inside her gloves, her hands were slick with sweat.

"What are you waiting for?" Hagan's voice drifted up to her. She could detect his outline against the wall of snow and saw he had stopped partway down the slope.

"I—I'll be down in a minute," she said. She hoped he'd mistake the quaver in her voice for an effect of the wind. She planted her pole and told herself this time she would ski down. Straight to him without stopping. Yes, the slope was steep, and there was little room for error in the narrow chute, but she'd skied steeper and narrower before. She had the skills to do this.

She leaned forward, ready to go, and a wave of dizziness made her lurch back. The image of herself falling, bouncing like a rag doll down the slope, filled her head. The sickening sensation of having no control vibrated through every nerve. Nausea gripped her, and she clenched her teeth until her jaw hurt.

"Is something wrong?" Hagan asked.

Yes! she wanted to shout. *I can't do this.* She had the skills, but she no longer had the nerve. That's what her coach had told her when she'd tried to rejoin the team after her recovery. *You've lost your nerve, Maddie. It happens after a bad injury sometimes.*

She'd wanted to race so badly, but all the desire in the world couldn't overcome the fear that left her shaking and weak.

"Then get down here!" Hagan shouted. "There is no other way off the mountain unless you want me to call Scott and tell him to send a snowmobile for you." His tone was teasing, as if he was dealing with a reluctant tourist.

She shut her eyes. No! She'd be a laughingstock among the patrollers if she had to ride a snowmobile down the mountain. She was a skier, dammit! And as a patroller, she was supposed to be able to ski all the terrain. If she couldn't ski, what else could she do with her life? Skiing was all she knew.

She took a deep breath, and shoved off, then half-skidded to the next turn. At every turn, she stopped and repeated the process, all the while fighting nausea and the sensation that she absolutely was going to fall, and maybe even die, before she got to the bottom.

"What are you looking at?" she demanded when she stopped beside Hagan. Though she couldn't see his eyes behind his goggles, his mouth was set in a frown.

"Are you sure you are okay?" he asked.

"Leave me alone and ski!" She wanted to hit him over the head with her ski pole, but that would mean lifting it off the ground and risking losing her balance.

He opened his mouth as if to reply, then turned and raced down the run. She stared after him, envious of the perfect form with which he executed turns and maneuvered in the narrow chute. Guys like him made it look easy. She'd been able to do that once. Until the accident, when all confidence had deserted her. That loss hurt more than all the pain of her physical injuries.

She made it down through sheer determination, fighting panic the whole way, her heart pounding and her limbs shaking. Hagan was waiting for her at the bottom, but she slid past him, not wanting to hear any more of his cutting remarks.

On less steep terrain now, she poured on the speed, anxious to get off the mountain altogether. Let Hagan write her up or fire her or whatever he wanted—there was no one here she might run into and she needed to burn off the adrenaline that left her shaky and sick to her stomach.

To his credit, he kept up with her. "Maddie, wait!" he called, but she ignored him. She had nothing to say to Mr. Hagan Ansdar. She'd fallen apart in front of him and no doubt the news would be all through patrol by tomorrow. She'd be lucky to have a job, much less any chance of salvaging her pride. Just when she'd thought she'd sunk as low as she could go by working as a patroller, she'd proven to herself that she didn't even have the guts to do that. Her life as a skier was over.

HAGAN WATCHED Maddie race away, confusion warring with anger. She had looked like a different woman up there on Peel. Gone was the graceful skier he had admired, replaced by a shaking, hostile amateur. If that was the true Maddie, she had no business on the mountain let alone on patrol.

She skidded to a halt outside the Gothic Center cafeteria, clicked out of her skis and hustled inside. Zephyr was emerging from the building and stared after her, then turned to Hagan. "What happened to her? She looked a little green."

"We went up on Peel to check out the powder," he said. "We got to the top of the run and she freaked."

"You took her down Peel? No wonder she flaked on you."

"What do you mean?" He brushed snow from his shoulders and frowned at his friend. "She ought to be able to ski double black. She was supposedly an Olympic-caliber skier."

"Yeah, but she had that horrific accident." Zephyr shook his head. "I bet it's like post-traumatic stress or something. You know, where soldiers flash back to battle and relive horrible stuff? She was probably up there remembering her accident."

Hagan stared at Zephyr. The man had such a stoner-rocker-boarder image he forgot sometimes that Zephyr was actually pretty smart. "I knew she had an accident. Was it really that bad?"

"Dude, it was sick! The video's on YouTube some-where. You should take a look." He glanced toward the door where Maddie had disappeared. "Truth? I'm sur-prised she ever got back on a pair of skis again."

HAGAN DID NOT SEE Maddie the rest of the day. He sus-pected she was avoiding him. He alternated between feeling guilty about talking her into skiing Peel, and anger that she had not spoken up and told him she was afraid to ski the steeps in these conditions.

Of course, in the same position, he would not have admitted he was afraid. But she was a woman. They were supposed to be better at admitting their true emotions, were they not?

After his shift he turned down Zephyr's invitation to check out a new band at a local club, and headed to his cabin. After feeding Fafner and heating soup for him-self, he logged onto the Internet and searched YouTube for "Skiing accident" and "Maddie Alexander."

The film was in color, apparently part of the video from television coverage of the event, one of the final World Cup races before the Olympics, in St. Moritz, Switzerland. Maddie, wearing the skintight one-piece red, white and blue racing uniform of the U.S. team and a blue helmet painted with clouds, popped out of the gate and barreled down a steep slope that glinted blue with ice.

Though the sun was shining at the top of the slope, halfway down she momentarily disappeared from view in a cloud of blowing snow. She skidded around a sharp turn and fought for control, miraculously righting herself and tucking tightly to regain speed.

She was a blur as she soared down another straight-away and into the next right turn. The steel-on-ice screech of ski edges scraping the hardpack rasped from the speakers. Hagan gripped the edge of the desk, his whole body tensed, his own muscles tightening, his body bracing as she took yet another curve at breath-taking speed.

Then she hit a jump and soared through the air. Too high, he could tell, and he sucked in his breath along with the spectators on the video as she hit the ice hard, at the wrong angle. Arms and legs flying, she bounced, then rolled like a crumpled wad of paper hurtling down the slope, hitting, rising, hitting again.

Hagan groaned as she came to a stop, arms and legs at unnatural angles. She was still. Absolutely still. The screen went black, yet he continued to stare, fighting nausea.

If he had not known better, he would have thought the woman in the video was now dead. How had she survived such a fall, much less come back to ski again?

He took a deep breath and sat back in his chair. No wonder she had freaked out up there on Peel. The snow swirling around her, the steep pitch and narrow chute were not that different from conditions the day of her career-ending accident.

So why had she not let him call for a snowmobile to take her down? He did not have to search hard for the answer to that question. He knew a little about pride himself.

He thought back to part of the conversation they had had at the Eldo, when he had spouted that nonsense about facing fears. As if he knew much about that. He was much better at taking the other advice he had given her—that sometimes it was better to avoid the fear-inducing situation altogether.

He had built a life for himself based on that one principle, a life that, though lacking in a certain warmth, left him in control of events and emotions. He knew all about maintaining control.

But Maddie might be able to teach him a thing or two about courage.

MADDIE DID HER BEST to avoid Hagan for the next few days. She was mortified that she'd fallen apart in front of him, and had no desire to hear any more comments about her supposed Olympic skiing abilities.

Maybe if she'd freaked in front of another woman, or any other man on the patrol, it wouldn't have been so bad. But Hagan was so infuriatingly *perfect*—a great skier and a skilled patroller with a reputation for always being cool in a crisis. The other patrollers looked up to him and of course, almost every woman he met drooled over him. She couldn't deny she'd done a little drooling herself, though that particular weakness annoyed her greatly. She didn't need Mr. Perfect reminding her of her own imperfections.

But Crested Butte was a small community, and she knew she'd run into him eventually. She told herself she'd keep things cool and cut him off at the knees if he even tried to bring up that day on the mountain. She succeeded in not seeing him for a week, but Friday night found her at the Eldo with Andrea, Scott and Lisa, Zephyr and Trish. She couldn't stop watching the door and sure enough, a little after eight o'clock, Hagan and Max walked in.

Maddie turned away and pretended interest in Zephyr's description of the new outfit he'd put together for his Free Skiing Championship debut. "What you wear says a lot about you," he said seriously.

"So does your outfit say 'this man is out of his mind?'" Trish said.

He grinned at her. "Crazy like a fox. I'll dazzle everyone with my threads, then blow their minds when I show my stuff on the mountain."

Trish rolled her eyes. "My mind is blown already, just contemplating it."

"Hey, where's Casey?" Trish asked as Max pulled out the chair beside her.

"She's helping Heather with some wedding stuff," Max said.

"Hers or Heather's?" Trish asked. Maddie had learned Dr. Ben Romney and Heather Allison, Casey's boss at the Crested Butte Chamber of Commerce, were due to wed in a few weeks.

Max shrugged. "To tell you the truth, I don't know. I leave all that up to her. I told her to just tell me when and where to show up and I'll be there, ready to say I do." He reached for a cup and the pitcher of beer in the center of the table. "It would be fine with me if we went to the courthouse in Gunnison and got it over with."

"A wedding should be more than a business transaction," Andrea said. "It should be a romantic day to remember."

"Women think like that," Scott said. "Men don't see what all the fuss is about."

"Maybe if it was conducted like a business transaction, people would be more realistic about what to expect from a marriage," Hagan said.

Scott laughed. "Like you'd know a lot about it, Casanova."

Hagan's face remained impassive. Maddie told herself she should quit looking at him, but she couldn't seem to help it. The man was a puzzle. Just when she thought she'd figured him out, he came up with some comment like that one about marriage and sent her thoughts spinning in a new direction.

As if feeling her gaze on him, he turned and for a split second, their eyes met. She quickly ducked her head, but not before registering the sadness in his expression.

No. She must have imagined it. Hagan was the always-sure-of-himself playboy. Mr. Perfect. What did he have to be sad about?

"Excuse me for a minute." She shoved back her chair and headed for the ladies' room. She needed a few minutes to pull herself together. To rehearse all the comebacks she'd thought of if Hagan said anything to her about what had happened up there on Peel.

In the ladies' room, she used the facilities, then lingered in front of the mirror, brushing her hair and touching up her lip gloss. Anything to delay going back out there. Not that she had anything to be afraid of. She was ready for anything Hagan had to say to her. As she'd discovered during her long period in rehab, anger could get her through all kinds of uncomfortable situations. Focus on the anger so that the hurt and shame didn't have a chance to creep in.

At last she put away the gloss and brush, slung her purse over one shoulder, and shoved out the door.

Straight into a solid wall of unyielding male muscle. Hagan steadied her with his hands on her elbows. "I was hoping I would have the chance to talk to you," he said.

She had to crane her neck to glare up at him, which spoiled the effect. It was tough to look fierce when you were scarcely five feet tall, especially when confronting a giant like Hagan. She tried to move out of his grasp, but he had a grip like iron. Short of hitting him with her purse and making a scene, she was stuck. "I don't want to talk to you," she said.

"We need to talk," he said, his voice firm. "About what happened on Peel."

Here it came. He was going to tell her she had no business being a patroller if she couldn't ski the double blacks. He was going to question why she'd been chosen for the Olympics in the first place, maybe even accuse her of trading on her reputation and that infamous *Sports Illustrated* cover to get her job with the resort.

"I apologize for taking you up there," he said. "I should have backed off when you told me the first time you did not want to go."

She blinked, all the angry words she'd been rehearsing stuck in her throat. He was *apologizing?* Mr. Perfect was admitting he was wrong?

He released one arm, but kept hold of the other and guided her gently toward the door. "Let us go somewhere we can talk. Alone."

Disarmed by his unexpected humility, she let him

lead her out the door, down the stairs and across the street to a new bistro that had opened on Elk Avenue. "The coffee here is almost as good as Trish's, and they have good desserts," Hagan said as they sat at a table for two near the front.

Maddie nodded, still dazed. She swallowed and found her voice. "I can ski those runs," she said. "I've done it before. It was just that morning, in those conditions…" Her voice faded and she looked away. She couldn't explain exactly what had happened there at the top of Peel, except that for a moment she'd been back on the course at St. Moritz, and the memory of her fall had overwhelmed her.

Hagan said nothing else until their order of coffee and crème brûlée was in front of them. He stirred sugar into his cup and regarded her with a sympathetic look. "I watched the video of your accident on YouTube. I had not realized before how horrible it was."

"YouTube?" She gave a weak laugh. "Figures it would end up there. Me and that guy from *The Wide World of Sports* who illustrated 'the agony of defeat.'" She'd watched that show as a kid and winced every time they'd replayed the anonymous skier's crash. Now she was the one making people wince.

"Zephyr said that day on Peel that maybe you were reliving what happened to you. Something like post-traumatic stress in soldiers."

"Zephyr knows what happened?" Did everyone know? Were they all discussing her behind her back and she had no idea?

"He is the only one. I did not tell anyone else." His voice was stern. "It was none of their business."

She relaxed a little and nodded. "Yes, I guess that's what happened. I looked down that run, all the swirling snow, and just…froze." She shuddered, remembering. She had never been so terrified in her life, absolutely paralyzed by fear.

"Why not leave skiing altogether?" Hagan asked. "Or be a tourist? Why take a job that puts you out there every day?"

She'd asked herself that question often enough, and always came up with the same answer. "Skiing is what I do. I was given a talent and I screwed it up." She swallowed hard. "I hoped being on patrol would help me figure out how to move past the fear—to get over it and go back to doing what I'm good at. And to… I guess I figured if I used my talent to help others, it would make up for that mistake." She'd spent a lot of time lying in her hospital bed, alternately reliving the accident and bargaining with God, as if the right combination of penance and practice would bring her old life back.

"It is a dangerous sport," he said. "What happened was not your fault."

She shook her head. "I was being reckless. Taking too many chances. I knew I had to pull off an exceptional time to win, so I went for it."

"That is what competitors do, is it not?"

"Yes." She scooped up a spoonful of the crème brûlée and studied it. "But my coach had warned me to be careful on that curve, to pull back a little. He knew I had a tendency to push and warned me not to press my luck. But I didn't listen."

"Your gamble could have paid off. You might have won."

"It didn't, and worse, it ended my career."

"You could have been hurt on Peel. I should not have let you continue when I saw what was happening."

She looked him in the eye, some of her earlier anger returning. "I'd like to have seen you try to stop me," she said. "It was my decision to go down that run, even if I didn't do it with the best form. I don't want anyone making allowances for me and don't you dare pity me."

He nodded, his expression serious. "Pity is not the word I think of when I think of you," he said.

"Oh? Good." She ate another bite of the dessert, then curiosity got the better of her. "What word do you think of?"

He paused, as if considering the question. "I think of words like grace. Determination. Courage."

"I wasn't very brave up there on Peel."

His eyes met hers again, so blue and clear and unblinking. Eyes that held no false flattery or flirtation. "There are different kinds of courage," he said. "And there are ways in which every one of us is a coward."

She didn't believe Hagan had ever been a coward; he was only saying that to make her feel better. But the knowledge warmed her more than all the hot coffee or fleece mittens ever could. She smiled. "Thanks," she said. "You're not such a bad guy after all. Even if you are a player."

He acknowledged this little dig with a nod. "Think what you will about my relationships with women," he said. "You are better off as my friend than you would be as my lover."

The sudden tightness in her chest at his words caught her off guard. Why would he say something like that, and use such a charged word—*lover?* Unless, perhaps, he'd been thinking about the possibility.

She tried to dismiss the thought outright, but could not quite let go of it. Hagan was a strikingly handsome man who was rumored to have had many lovers, which implied a certain skill. She, on the other hand, could count her own serious relationships on the fingers of one hand. What would it be like to have a man like Hagan as her lover? She felt flushed and out of breath at the idea.

Of course she didn't want Hagan as her lover. He was the last man she'd ever consider.

But she couldn't quite ignore the small voice in the back of her head that whispered, *Liar.*

Chapter Four

The next week was college ski week at the resort. Hundreds of young men and women descended on the area to ski, snowboard and party. Patrol stayed busy treating injuries, giving directions to lost visitors and dealing with the occasional unruly drunk.

Maddie was no longer avoiding Hagan, but they were both too busy to do more than exchange greetings in passing. The Tuesday after their conversation at the restaurant, she and Andrea spent the afternoon marking hazards on slopes that had turned icy in the intense sunshine and above-normal temperatures. "So what's the dumbest question you've been asked today?" Andrea asked.

"I'll have to think about it a minute," Maddie said. "What's yours?"

Andrea grinned. "A woman asked me if a snow cat was anything like a mountain lion."

Maddie laughed. "Actually, that's kind of cute." She pounded one end of a section of orange snow fence into the snow with a mallet while Andrea worked on the other end. "Yesterday I had a guy ask me why we didn't make the moguls more even," Maddie said after a moment. "I didn't get it at first, then I realized he thought we had some special machine that made the moguls. I had to explain that ungroomed snow naturally forms those hummocks when a lot of people ski down it." She shook her head. "I don't think he believed me."

They were packing up their tools, ready to move on to the next hazard on their list when two young men approached them. "Good afternoon, ladies," the taller of the two said. He had sun-bleached brown hair and a smile that any orthodontist would have been proud of. "Y'all live around here, don't you?" he asked.

"Yes," Andrea said. She offered a smile in return. Maddie hung back a little, wondering if they were going to have another candidate for the tourist question hall of fame.

"Then maybe you can help us out," Handsome Smile continued. "I'm Greg and this is my buddy, Evan."

Evan nodded and Maddie returned the greeting, still wondering where this was leading.

"We want to know where the best place is to get a drink in town," Greg said. "Where the locals hang out."

"That would be the Eldo," Andrea said. "It's down on Elk Avenue in town."

"Cool." Greg looked at Andrea, then Maddie, then back again to Andrea, his smile never wavering. "So, you ladies go there and it's good?"

"Pretty good." Andrea shrugged. "Nothing special, just a nice place."

Greg looked around them. A steady stream of skiers and boarders zipped past, and gathered in groups of two and three along the margins of the run to talk, rest or merely enjoy the sun. "This is our first time here," he said. "It's a great place." He looked back at them. "How long have you worked here?"

"This is my second year," Andrea said.

"Cool job, huh?"

"We like it." She glanced at Maddie, who nodded. She was trying to decide if Andrea was into this guy or merely playing him along.

"So, what time do you get off?" Greg asked. "Maybe the two of you could meet us at the Eldo for a drink."

"Maybe we'll see you there," Andrea said. "We volunteered to be in the torchlight parade tonight, though."

"What's the torchlight parade?" Evan, a stockier guy with reddish-brown hair, spoke for the first time.

"Every Friday and Saturday night a bunch of us ski down the front side carrying torches," Andrea explained. "It's quite a spectacle."

"Cool," Greg said. He glanced at Evan. "Maybe we'll stick around for that and we could meet up afterward."

"Maybe." Andrea's radio crackled. "I have to get back to work now," she said, with an apologetic look.

"Yeah. Thanks." Greg slid downhill a foot or so then stopped. "See you around."

"See you around," Andrea echoed.

Maddie stared after the two men. "Did you just make a date with that guy?" she asked when she was sure Evan and Greg were out of earshot.

"Not really." Andrea stowed her mallet in her pack. "But I wouldn't mind seeing him again. He's cute."

"Does that kind of thing happen much?" Maddie asked.

"What kind of thing?"

"Strangers coming up and flirting with you." Hagan was the only patroller she could think of who routinely got that sort of attention—from female skiers and boarders only, of course.

"Not all the time, but sometimes," Andrea said. She shouldered her pack. "Just like women get off on guys in uniform, it's a turn-on for some men, too."

Maddie absorbed this information. So there were benefits to this job she hadn't anticipated. Not that she was interested in a bunch of college guys. At twenty-eight, she was too old for them, and she wasn't really interested in getting involved with anyone right now. Between recovering from her accident, dealing with the disappointment of forced retirement and figuring out what to do with her life, she hadn't dated anyone in almost two years.

She kept thinking one day her libido would wake up, but so far it remained sadly dormant.

Except, of course, for the heightened awareness she felt when she was with Hagan. She told herself this was only because he was the type of man who would interest any woman. There was something about the combination of good looks, overt masculinity and Teutonic inscrutableness that was as tempting as a hot fudge sundae.

And every bit as bad for her, she reminded herself. Hagan had been right when he'd said he could be a good friend to a woman, but a terrible boyfriend. The fact that he had enough insight to realize this added another layer to his character. He might be a player, but he was far from shallow.

The rest of the day she was more attuned to the admiring glances of men they passed and what might be attempts at flirtation from some of these same men. Why hadn't she noticed this before? Was it because she'd been so intent on settling into the duties of her new job, because of the additional influx of single young men to the resort this week—or because she herself was suddenly giving off vibes that said "available"?

After the ski lifts shut down and patrol made its final sweep of the runs, Andrea and Maddie joined Scott, Eric and Marcie at Firehouse Grill for a quick supper before the torchlight parade. The restaurant, operated by local firefighters, claimed to have the best pizza and wings around.

"How are you liking patrol?" Marcie asked Maddie as they dove into their food.

"I like it okay," Maddie said. She'd gotten off to a rough start with her meltdown on Peel, but she'd settled down since then and was growing accustomed to the routine. She was trying hard to avoid pining for her racing days, since that only depressed her. She was even beginning to like some aspects of her new job. "I feel like I know the mountain better now," she said. "And I know more what to expect."

"You're doing a good job," Scott said. "You're good with the public and that's a lot of it."

The praise sent a warm glow through her. She had so much less experience than the other patrollers; it was good to know Scott thought she was pulling her weight. And the idea that they liked and respected her for herself, and not for the medals she'd won or records she'd broken, was new and gratifying.

"It must be a big change from being on the Olympic team," Eric said, helping himself to another slice of pizza.

The glow faded with this reminder of what might have been. "I never actually got to the Olympics," she said. "But this is different from my years on the U.S. ski team. For one thing, I've never skied the same place every day all winter."

"I hope you don't get bored here," Andrea said.

"What's boring is skiing the same run over and over," Maddie said. "That's pretty much what I did on the team. Well, one run at each venue. We never really had the opportunity to get to know a resort the way I'm getting to know Crested Butte."

"Where is home for you?" Marcie asked.

"I grew up in Vermont, near Stowe," she said. "But my parents live in Scottsdale and my brother moved out to Southern California." She wrinkled her nose. "Neither of those places have snow, so I can't see ever living there." She shrugged. "I guess I'll have to figure out later where home is."

She'd spent so many years traveling for months at a time that the idea of actually staying in one place for maybe the rest of her life was still something she couldn't quite wrap her mind around. It was one more question she needed to answer to complete the as-yet-undeveloped picture of her future.

After supper, the five friends rode the Red Lady Express lift up to the top and joined the other resort employees and friends lining up for the parade. This was the first time Maddie had participated in the event, and she was looking forward to taking part.

While she was waiting to collect her torch she heard a familiar softly accented voice and turned to see Hagan standing off to one side.

She started to call to him to join her, then saw that he wasn't alone. A tall woman with olive skin, waist-length dark hair and exotic features had one hand on his arm and smiled up at him with an expression that defined the word *smoldering*.

Maddie quickly looked away, trying to ignore the pinched feeling in her chest. Maybe the pizza had been too spicy.

"I see Hagan has a new admirer." Andrea skied over to Maddie. "Why is it all his women look like models?"

In spite of her determination not to, Maddie glanced back at Hagan and the woman. Miss Exotic was standing even closer to him now. If either of them tried to ski away, they'd both end up falling over. Maddie wasn't proud of the pleasure the idea gave her.

"Just once I'd like to see him with an ordinary-looking woman," Andrea said. "I hate to think he's really so shallow."

"I don't think Hagan's shallow." Maddie forced herself to face forward again. The man who had shown so much understanding of what had happened to her that day on Peel had more depth than most people she met. But for whatever reason, when it came to the women in his life, Hagan sought out the superficial. It was almost as if he was playing a role—pretending relationships didn't really matter to him.

And maybe they didn't. Maybe that was the one flaw in his perfect character. The idea did little to ease the ache in her chest.

"Everybody grab a torch," Mark Luan, director of mountain operations, instructed. "Do we have a volunteer to lead the way down?"

"I'll do it." Maddie grabbed up her torch and brandished it. Leading the parade sounded like fun. Besides, she was eager to put some distance between herself and Hagan and his flavor of the moment.

She and Andrea were chosen to lead a line of skiers, each holding a torch. They'd begin on opposite sides of the top of the run ending at the base area, where a crowd of spectators had gathered. They'd criss-cross back and forth across the snow, the two lines weaving in and out of one another, creating patterns of light and an impressive spectacle. From below, it looked easy, but every skier had to pay attention, time his or her turns and avoid running into any other skier, falling, or catching anything on fire with the flaming torch.

Maddie held her torch high and waited for the signal from Mark. Outside the short reach of the torchlight, the night was black velvet. The air was sharp with cold and filled with the pungent scents of woodsmoke and lighter fluid from the gas-fed torches. The freshly groomed snow rolled out before her in a white carpet.

Mark blew a sharp blast on the whistle and Maddie shoved off. Her skis glided over the corduroy ridges of powder, gradually picking up speed as the steepness of the slope increased. She leaned her body into the turn, keeping the torch high, and met Andrea near the middle of the run. She had a brief impression of her roommate's smiling face before they passed each other and headed toward the far side of the run.

At every turn, Maddie could see the other skiers out

of the corner of her eye, weaving ribbons of torchlight across the mountain. As they picked up speed toward the bottom of the run, she heard music, and the low murmur of the spectators.

Were Hagan and Miss Exotic skiing together? Did they have plans to do more than ski later?

She shook her head, banishing the thought, determined to think only of the moment—of how wonderful it felt to float down the darkened slope, the torch hissing overhead, casting wild shadows, the squeak of her skis gliding over the surface, the sureness of her body with every turn, the invigorating cold and the warm glow of light.

The run was over too soon. At the bottom she extinguished her torch and joined some other patrollers around a table set with hot chocolate and cookies. "So, what'd you think?" Andrea asked as she and Maddie helped themselves to chocolate.

"That was a blast," Maddie said. "I want to do it again."

"It's a great way to start the weekend," Andrea agreed. She raised her head and looked around. "Now if we could only find a couple of hunky college guys…"

"Hey, there you are!" As if on cue, Greg emerged from the crowd and headed toward them. Evan followed behind. "We've been looking for you two," Greg said.

"Well, here we are." Andrea smiled at them. "What did you guys think of the parade?"

"It was awesome," Greg said.

"Is that hard to do?" Evan moved beside Maddie and addressed her. "I mean to ski with a torch like that?"

"Not really," Maddie said. "It was fun." Even though

Evan seemed like a nice guy, she really didn't have any interest in spending the evening with him.

Just then, she spotted Hagan and Miss Exotic. They were holding hands, moving toward the tables of refreshments. In fact, they were headed right toward her. A few seconds more and he was bound to see her. She didn't think she'd be able to stand it if he felt compelled to introduce her to his latest conquest.

Impulsively, she grabbed Evan's hand. "Tell me about yourself," she said, with her most inviting smile.

He blinked, then grinned. "What do you want to know?"

"Everything," she said. At least now when Hagan saw her, he'd realize he wasn't the only one who'd found companionship for a Friday night.

HAGAN SPOTTED MADDIE as he headed toward the refreshment table with Veronica in tow. He had met the shapely Brazilian beauty over coffee that afternoon, and she had announced her intention to spend the rest of her vacation with him. He had not found the idea objectionable; Veronica was intelligent, witty and definitely easy on the eyes.

But he momentarily forgot all about the beautiful woman beside him when he saw Maddie holding hands with a shaggy-haired guy who wore a gold ring in one ear. He stopped and stared at the two of them. What was Maddie doing with that kid? Was he even old enough to legally buy a drink? Yet, she was smiling at him, head tilted slightly to one side, as if she were pondering the answer to a question. She laughed at something the kid said, and the sound floated to Hagan over the conversation of the crowd. He tensed, an uncomfortable emotion very like anger coiling in his gut.

"What is wrong? Why are you squeezing my hand so hard?" Veronica pulled away and scowled at him. "You're hurting me."

"Sorry." Hagan shoved both hands into the pockets of his ski jacket and gave her an apologetic look. "I was distracted for a moment."

"Oh?" Veronica raised one perfectly arched eyebrow. "What did you see to make you squeeze the life out of my hand?"

Hagan shook his head. "Nothing." But he could not keep from glancing at Maddie and the boy again.

"Ahh," Veronica said knowingly. She smiled, a seductive expression. "Is it the woman or the man she's with who upsets you so?"

"Neither." He turned his back to Maddie and her companion and forced himself to focus on the woman before him.

Veronica rewarded him with an even warmer smile. She slipped her hand into the crook of his arm and pressed her body close to his. The expensive fur-trimmed parka she wore did little to disguise her figure. Hagan appreciated a woman who was candid about what she wanted from him. Veronica was interested in a few days of fun to enliven her vacation. She expected they would have a good time, then say goodbye, with no regrets—exactly what Hagan himself wanted.

Ordinarily, at this point in the evening he would have suggested they skip the refreshments and retire to her condo to continue getting to know one another better. He opened his mouth to make just such a proposal, but the words were not there. He stared at Veronica's perfectly shaped face, her full lips and expertly made-up eyes and felt…nothing. Not the faintest stirring of desire or even interest. The thought of spending the evening trying to manufacture emotion where none existed pained him.

Veronica's brown eyes clouded. "Why are you looking at me that way?" she demanded.

He realized he had stared at her so long without saying anything that he was bordering on rudeness. He shook his head, hoping to clear it, and took a step away from her. "I apologize," he said. "I am not myself tonight. It would be better if we said goodbye now."

"Goodbye?" She released her hold on him, eyes bright, her face animated with anger. "You have occupied my time all afternoon, only to say goodbye now? What kind of a trick is this?"

Hagan could feel rage radiating from her like heat from a smoldering fire. He had expected no less and could not blame her. His attentions all afternoon had promised things he now found himself unable to deliver. While he might have faked his way through the evening well enough, he would not lower himself or her to such depths. Better to beg off now while she still had the opportunity to find someone who would truly enjoy her companionship. "I was wrong," he said, his open hands extended in a gesture of apology. "I have too much on my mind to be good company tonight."

Her anger cooled slightly and she leaned toward him. "I am sure I would be able to distract you from whatever is bothering you," she said.

Maybe. But he was not in the mood to be distracted.

"Would you like me to take you back to your condo before I leave you?" he asked.

He was fairly certain that the words she hurled at him would translate to profanity in any language. The hatred in her eyes would have reduced a lesser man to cinders. As it was, several of those around them took a step backward. She pulled her parka more tightly around her, tossed her head, and stalked away still muttering under her breath.

Hagan ignored the curious looks of bystanders and turned once more toward where Maddie and the kid had been standing. But they were gone now. Not that it was any of his concern, he reminded himself. Maddie could do as she liked; his irritable mood this evening had nothing to do with her.

Of course, the fact that he could not stop thinking about her lately irritated him. What was it about the woman that made her so hard to get out of his mind? She was not the most beautiful woman he had ever encountered, though she was certainly attractive. She was not flirtatious or provoking. Outwardly, there was nothing particularly remarkable about her. Yet ever since they met he had found it difficult to forget about her. Even when he was with other women he found himself thinking of her, finding fault with his companions in a way he had never done before. It was maddening!

In any case, he was poor company for anyone tonight. He would go back to his cabin and rest. Maybe he was coming down with something—some virus that made him obsess about a woman he had no business thinking so much about.

Chapter Five

The third week of January blew into Crested Butte with a major snowstorm that made the skiers and boarders rejoice and left everyone else grumbling about all the white stuff to be shoveled. Maddie was no longer addressed as "the new girl" among the patrollers, as everyone had learned her name, and she had signed up for additional training in avalanche awareness, with the idea of eventually being assigned to the avalanche control squad. She hoped the added excitement of working with explosives would help replace the adrenaline rush of racing she still missed. Who said men were the only ones who liked to flirt with danger?

The only dark spot in the otherwise pleasant routine into which she'd settled was the appearance of hearts and cupids in the windows of stores all over town. Even the ski resort was decorated in shades of red and pink, the sentiments of Be Mine and Happy Valentine's Day displayed everywhere.

Even a person who wasn't interested in a serious relationship couldn't help but be dismayed at the prospect of a February 14 unattached. But when she shared her feelings with Andrea as they walked down Elk Avenue one evening, her roommate only laughed. "It's almost a month to Valentine's," she said. "Plenty of time to find someone to send you flowers."

"I don't want someone to send me flowers," Maddie said. And the idea of suddenly embarking on a flurry of dating made her shudder. Her one date with Evan, the college guy, had been an exercise in awkwardness. Not only was he seven years younger than her, but they had little in common. Conversation had been a struggle and she'd been relieved when he'd ended the evening early.

"In fact, I don't want anyone," she continued. "I just hate the idea of a holiday that makes it seem as if there's something wrong with anyone who's single."

"It's not as bad as all that," Andrea said. "Valentine's Day isn't an attack on singles. How can you complain about a holiday that celebrates something positive like love?"

"You're right," Maddie said. "But I wish the hearts and flowers weren't taking over everything."

"You'll feel better when you've had one of Trish's special mochas," Andrea said as she pushed open the door to the coffee shop.

The interior of the shop was fragrant with the scents of cinnamon and chocolate. Trish looked up from arranging pastries in a display case and greeted them. "Hey! I've been hoping you two would stop by." She rummaged in a drawer beneath the cash register and pulled out two red envelopes.

Maddie groaned. "Please tell me that's not a valentine," she said, as Trish offered her one of the envelopes.

"Don't mind her," Andrea said, accepting her own envelope. "She doesn't like Valentine's Day."

"It's not a valentine, I promise," Trish said. "It's an invitation to a shower I'm throwing for Heather Allison."

Maddie slit open her envelope and studied the cartoon of frogs dancing with umbrellas.

"I know you don't know Heather that well," Trish said. "But you know her fiancé, Dr. Ben, and you're friends with the rest of us. It's going to be a fun party, and I didn't want you to be left out."

"Thanks," Maddie said. She was touched by Trish's thoughtfulness. "I'd love to come."

"Me, too," Andrea said. "Sounds like a good time."

"I'm closing up the shop next Monday night and having the party here," Trish said. "Neither Heather nor Ben really need anything, so the theme is gag gifts and fun stuff. And it's chicks only so we can let our hair down. I'm going to have drinks and lots of yummy goodies."

"It's really sweet of you to do that," Maddie said.

"I was in the mood for a party," Trish said. "Besides, the closer it gets to the wedding day, the more nervous Heather becomes. She's driving us all crazy. I thought this would help relieve some of the tension."

"When is the wedding?" Maddie asked.

"Valentine's Day," Trish said.

Andrea laughed. "Good day for a wedding." She nudged Maddie with her elbow.

"Yeah," Maddie said. If two people truly loved each other, then she could see how Valentine's might be a meaningful holiday. But since she didn't have even the prospect of love in her life, she reserved the right to remain disgruntled.

THE FOLLOWING SATURDAY, Maddie and Hagan were assigned to patrol together. This was fast becoming her favorite part of the job—being paid to ski runs, looking for people in need of assistance, on the alert for potential hazards or troublemakers and generally interacting with resort guests. She'd discovered she had a knack for dealing with people. Maybe all those years of hanging out with the varied personalities of other racers on the circuit and her occasional dealings with the press had given her some useful real-world skills after all.

She wasn't sure how she felt about spending the day working with Hagan, however. On one hand, she welcomed the chance to get to know him better. On the other, he was still the player she'd seen at the torchlight parade with a gorgeous female on his arm.

Not that she cared who he dated, she reminded herself. But didn't he care that his friends saw him as such a dog? She'd glimpsed a genuinely nice person behind his player facade—why didn't he let more of that side of himself show?

The man was an enigma and she saw it as a challenge to figure out what made him tick. Today was as good an opportunity as any. "What do you do in the summer?" she asked as they headed up the lift after a run through Paradise Bowl. A storm last night had laid down a fresh blanket of powder, while bright sunshine today made for perfect skiing conditions. She had to rein in the urge to fly down the smooth, gently rolling terrain.

"I work for the forest service as a seasonal ranger," he said.

"And what does a seasonal ranger do?" she prompted.

"Whatever they tell me." His smile was rueful. "Everything from cleaning portable toilets to leading guided nature hikes to clearing brush."

"How long have you been doing this?" *So like a man to never volunteer any additional information,* she thought. By now a woman would have told all about how she got the job, her favorite and least-favorite things about it and what the uniform looked like.

"Six years."

As long as he'd been on ski patrol, then. "Then you enjoy the work?"

"Yes." He glanced at her. "You sound skeptical."

She hadn't meant for that to come through in her voice. Had she done a poorer-than-usual job of hiding her feelings, or was Hagan particularly perceptive? "It just seems like an…impermanent way to make a living," she said. "I mean, you're obviously smart and capable. Hardworking." She struggled to say what she meant. "Six years at two basically part-time jobs is a lot."

"You mean, why am I not out there climbing the corporate ladder and making a real living?" he asked. His face was calm and there was no anger in his voice. Maybe she wasn't the first person to pose these questions.

"Well…yes," she said. Of course, she was one to talk. She didn't have a career or prospects of one, though she couldn't see working patrol for the rest of her life. She didn't even know what she'd be doing this summer. In the past, she'd have spent the warmer months training in South America, but that wasn't an option this year. What else could she do that didn't involve skiing?

She looked away from Hagan. At this point on the lift ride she had a good view of the half-pipe. Snowboarders and skiers soared above the edge of the icy tube, then raced to the bottom like BBs bouncing off the sides of a bottle.

"Not everyone is cut out for the corporate life," he said. "I prefer to find work I enjoy."

Work with no pressure. No stress. Not unlike his brief relationships with women who passed through town. She could see the appeal, though this picture of a man who divorced himself from the trappings of success didn't fit with the meticulous way he carried out his duties on ski patrol.

"After all," he added, "I have no one to support but myself."

They reached the top of the lift and exited the chair. Maddie contemplated his words as they headed down a run named Ruby Chief. Hagan was certainly doing everything he could to make sure he had only himself to support. Maybe that was the real point of his love 'em and leave 'em approach to dating. But wasn't that kind of life sort of…empty? Didn't he want more? Didn't he want love?

"What did you do before you came to Crested Butte?" she asked when she caught up with him at a point where the run branched off.

"I had a boring corporate job." Before she could ask more he took off to the left, and she had to hurry to keep up with him.

Midway down the run, they stopped to check on a girl who had fallen. Once they'd made sure she was all right, they gave directions to an older couple who were trying to find the Paradise restaurant, then headed toward the East River lift.

In the lift chair again, Hagan turned to Maddie. "Now it is my turn to question you. What are your plans for the summer?"

"I don't know. I haven't thought that far ahead." She'd avoided the question because her prospects for the future seemed so empty.

"And after that?" he continued. "Do you have plans for a career or will you be a slacker like me?"

She flushed, then realized he was teasing. His eyes sparked with laughter, though his expression remained severe. "Maybe," she said. "I'll give it a try. You could give me pointers."

"There are people who could tutor you better than me," he said. "Zephyr, for instance, is an expert at cobbling together part-time jobs and temporary living arrangements."

"I know people make fun of Zephyr and his big dreams," she said. "But at least he's dreaming."

At the top of the lift, she slid off the chair and skied ahead of him. All her dreams had died on that run in St. Moritz and she hadn't been able to come up with any new ones since. She'd searched and found nothing that held her interest, nothing she wanted to do.

The feeling of living a life on hold was frustrating. Even Hagan, with his intentionally low-key lifestyle, had an unspoken goal—to avoid any complications in his life.

Maddie craved complications, if only to point her in some direction—to give her some clue as to where to go from here. She wanted another opportunity to get her life right, but part of her was afraid there was no such thing as a second chance.

MADDIE WAS IN A BETTER mood the evening of Heather's shower. Trish had transformed her coffee shop into a scarlet boudoir. The tables, chairs and even the walls were draped in red fabric. A disco ball suspended in the center of the ceiling reflected light from dozens of candles arranged on the front counter, the tables and shelves on the walls. The guest of honor, seated in a chair marked with a large silver bow, looked alternately thrilled and on the verge of tears. "Oh, Trish, it's absolutely gorgeous," she said, dabbing at her eyes with her fingertips.

Trish handed her a box of tissues. "Don't cry yet," she said. "We haven't even gotten to the gifts."

"I'm just so emotional these days," Heather said, pulling several tissues from the box.

"I think a woman about to be married to the man of her dreams would be happier," teased Patti, who worked at the Teocali Tamale.

"Trust me," said Casey, Heather's best friend and coworker. "If she gets any happier, we're going to have to tie weights to her ankles to keep her from floating away."

"Makes me glad I don't work at the Chamber," Andrea said as she helped herself to a chocolate truffle from the tray Trish had set out. "Two brides-to-be in one place might be a little much."

"I don't know about that," Casey said. "We're thinking of using the idea to recruit more help. Come to work for the Chamber of Commerce and end up engaged."

"But you didn't meet Max because of your job at the Chamber," Heather protested. "He's your landlord. And I've known Ben for years—it's merely coincidence that we both work at the Chamber."

"Still, remind me to never volunteer there," Trish said. "Just in case it *is* contagious."

"Oh, Trish," Heather said. "Don't tell me you're not interested in getting married one of these days."

"I'm not opposed to marriage," Trish said. "I just don't believe there are any men in this town worth marrying. Except for those who are already taken," she added with a smile for Casey and Heather.

Maddie thought Trish was being a little harsh. She'd met plenty of nice men in Crested Butte—though the only one who had sparked any real reaction in her was the one perhaps most unsuitable for a future mate. Apparently, a lifetime of risk taking translated into a penchant for being drawn to risky men. She could add that to the list of things she needed to change if she was ever going to enjoy a so-called normal life.

"I don't know about that, either," Casey said. She turned to Maddie. "When I first came to town, it seemed as if every woman I met warned me not to fall for Max. They said he wasn't the marrying kind." She grinned. "Guess I proved them wrong."

"He simply had to meet the right woman," Trish said. She looked around at her guests. "Everyone have plenty to eat and drink?" she asked.

Everyone nodded and agreed they had plenty.

"Great," Trish said. "Then let's get to the gifts."

Trish and Casey piled a mound of colorful packages in front of Heather, who oohed and ahhed over the bright wrappings. Her joy soon turned to dismay and mirth as she opened the first box to reveal a much abbreviated nightgown. "Oh, my," she said, blushing. She folded the gown and set it aside. "Well, I'm sure Ben will enjoy that."

The next gift was a large pink whistle and a bag of chocolate kisses. "So you can train him right," Patti said.

Andrea's gift was his and hers silk boxer shorts, which delighted Heather. "I can't let Emma see them, though," she said, referring to her twelve-year-old daughter. "She'll make fun of me. She thinks two *old* people like us in love is embarrassing."

"Everything parents do is embarrassing at that age," Casey said. She handed Heather a box wrapped in silver-and-pink foil. "This one's from me."

Heather tore into the paper and pulled out a pair of hand-blown goblets. "Casey, they're gorgeous!" she exclaimed.

"That's not a joke gift," Trish chided.

Casey grinned. "I was going to get you something funny, but then I saw these and knew you'd love them."

"I do love them. And I love you, too." Heather looked around at them. "Thank you, all of you."

Maddie was surprised to feel her own eyes sting with tears at this sentiment. It was as if Heather had embraced them all in a hug, and Maddie had not been left out of that circle.

"To Heather and Ben." Casey raised her glass.

"To Heather and Ben." The others joined the toast. Trish refilled their glasses and they returned to opening gifts. Heather received a vintage copy of *The Newlywed Game* Maddie had found in a local thrift store, a collection of massage oils, more lingerie and a book entitled *Advice for the Young Wife* from the fifties that left them all weak with laughter.

It was after midnight when the party finally broke up. "This was wonderful," Maddie told Trish before she left. "Thank you so much for inviting me."

"You're one of the local gang now," Trish said. "I wouldn't think of not including you."

Maddie fumbled putting on her gloves, not wanting Trish to see how much this simple declaration moved her. Such gestures of friendship were the kind of thing Trish and the others seemed to take for granted, but they were still a novelty to Maddie. She'd spent the last ten years in a highly competitive world of professional skiing. Though she had spent that time largely in the company of other women near her age, the ever-present competition among even the members of the same team for the few cherished spots on the winners' podium made close friendships difficult, if not impossible.

Trish, Andrea, Casey, Heather and the others had so readily welcomed her into their circle. For the first time in her life, Maddie felt she was making real friends here. It was one more benefit of coming to Crested Butte that she hadn't anticipated. Knowing she had gained this gift lessened the hurt of all she had lost.

HAGAN STUDIED the line of hot dogs suspended from a piece of string stretched the length of the alley behind

Max's snowboard and bike shop. "Tell me again what this is about," he asked Max, who crouched beside him at the entrance to the alley, one hand wrapped in the collar of Casey's black retriever, Lucy. The pup stared at the hot dogs, drooling a little.

"We're training for the Winter Carnival dog races," Max said. He smoothed his hand down the dog's broad back. "I'm trying to teach her to ignore the hot dogs and race to me at the end."

Hagan eyed the drooling pup and shook his head. "I do not think that is going to happen. She likes hot dogs better than she likes you."

"Don't listen to him, girl," Max said, addressing the dog. "You can do this. And if you win, there's a steak in it for you, I promise." He looked up at Hagan again. "Hold on to her for a minute, will you? I'm going down to the other end of the alley. When I say so, let her go."

Hagan knelt and took hold of the dog. She greeted him with a big kiss on the side of his face, her whole body vibrating with joy. He laughed and ducked out of the way of a second swipe of her tongue.

"All right," Max called from the other end of the alley. "Let her go."

Hagan released his hold on the dog at the same time Max whistled for her. She took off toward him, then veered off course a few yards down the alley. She snapped at a hot dog, pulling it free of the string, and devoured it in three bites, then moved on to the next treat.

"Lucy, no!" Max called.

The dog wagged her tail and ate even faster.

Max ran up and grabbed her before she could eat all

the hot dogs. "She still needs work," he said. "Maybe I should use fewer hot dogs."

"Maybe you should quit while you are ahead," Hagan said.

He helped Max remove the remaining weiners and deposit them in a plastic bag. "Have you figured out your costume for the Disco on Ice party?" Max asked. In true Crested Butte style, the Winter Carnival featured a disco-themed party at the local ice rink, yet another opportunity for locals to raid their costume closets and dress their wackiest. Newcomers often shook their heads at the town's penchant for costume parties. Rarely a month went by without some sort of celebration requiring themed dress. Hagan himself had been taken aback at first, but had quickly gotten into the spirit of things and now, like any socially adept local, had a collection of strange and outrageous outfits. There was something very freeing about assuming an alter ego for one night.

But this time he felt no enthusiasm for the prospect of dressing up and acting crazy. "I do not know if I am going to go to the party," he said.

"Not go?" Max straightened, clearly alarmed at the idea. "Why not? You know these things are always a blast."

Hagan shrugged. "I am not in the mood for partying."

"What's up?" Max asked. "Something on your mind?"

"Nothing in particular." He did not know how to explain the restlessness that had plagued him these past few weeks. "I am thinking maybe I need a change of scenery. I might take a trip."

"Where to? And what about your job with ski patrol?"

"I might be able to negotiate a leave of absence. Maybe I will go someplace warm. Or maybe back to Norway." The fact that Norway even entered his mind surprised him. He had not been back home in over five years.

"Why not wait until mud season, when everyone else leaves town?" Max asked.

"I could." It would save hassles with his job. Truthfully, he did not know what he wanted, only that he could not shake the feeling that something in his life needed to change.

"Hey there!" Casey waved to them from the back steps of the apartments over Max's store. A pretty blonde who had come to Crested Butte from Chicago about a year ago, she had done the impossible and transformed Max, an affirmed bachelor, into a cheerful husband-to-be. Hagan still marveled at times at how quickly the change had taken place. He would have sworn Max was as set against marriage as Hagan, and yet almost from the moment he had laid eyes on Casey, he had been a changed man.

Casey hurried down the steps toward them. "Did Lucy pass the hot dog test?"

"I don't think she passed up even one," Max said. He looked down at the dog. "Maybe we should start with getting her to run the course without the temptation first."

"She's a smart dog. I'm sure she'll get the hang of it." She bent to pat the dog, then turned to Hagan. "What are you up to today?"

"I came into town to see if Max is interested in

going with me and Zephyr on some training runs tomorrow or the next day. He wants to spend some time over on the Head Wall where the competition will be held next month."

Casey gave Max a worried look. "Please don't do any crazy stunts."

"I'll take it easy," Max promised. "Zephyr's the crazy one. But not as crazy as people think sometimes. He knows what he's doing on a board."

"I feel better knowing Hagan will be there," she said. "At least he knows first aid. I guess the only thing better would be to have Ben there."

"Doctor Ben does not ski double blacks," Hagan said. The good doctor was strictly an intermediate skier.

"Then I'd say he's the smart one." Casey grinned. "I almost forgot. Heather wanted me to remind you that you and Hagan and Ben have a fitting for your tuxes in Gunnison Friday afternoon."

Max groaned. "Is she sure she doesn't want to take my suggestion and have everyone wear Hawaiian shirts? The women could wear tropical print dresses. The whole thing could be a Valentine's luau."

Casey shook her head. "I didn't buy that idea for our wedding, either. So don't forget the tux fitting. It'll be good practice for you."

Max sent Hagan a pleading look. Hagan shook his head. "I have no problem wearing a tuxedo." He grinned. "I am told I look good in it."

"Some woman probably said that," Max groused. "And only because she wanted something from you."

"I have to go," Casey said. "I have to get these ad proofs to the newspaper before they close." She stood on tiptoe and kissed Max on the lips. He wrapped his arms around her and extended the kiss.

Hagan looked away. Such displays usually did not bother him; he had come to expect them from the lovebirds. But today he felt an unfamiliar gnawing in his gut. He might have even called it jealousy.

Once upon a time, as all fairy tales began, he had been on the receiving end of such kisses. He had been young and foolish as only a man who fancies himself in love could be. Happiness was his, but in the end it was a sham.

Other people seemed able to find love, but he had proved he was no good judge. Better to make a good life on his own than to count on someone else for something they could not give.

Chapter Six

Dressed in a vintage pair of shiny green bell-bottom trousers, platform shoes and a green-and-gold polyester blouse with wide lapels, her hair flipped back in a Farrah Fawcett do, Maddie alternated between feeling ridiculous and energized. What with always training for a race or recovering from injuries, she'd had few opportunities to really cut loose and act crazy. Maybe the Winter Carnival Disco on Ice party was the perfect time to discover her inner wild woman.

"I can't believe how many people are here," she said to Andrea as the two of them pressed their way into the packed Nordic Center Ice Rink.

"Oh, everybody comes to these things," Andrea said. She wore hot pants with suspenders, boots and a white turtleneck. "Any excuse for a party. Besides, it's for a good cause."

"Right." Maddie had almost forgotten that all the proceeds from this and other Winter Carnival events went to the Crested Butte Avalanche Center. The center provided daily reports on avalanche risks and snow conditions in the backcountry throughout the area. "Oh, there's Trish!" She waved to their friend, whose Laura Ashley peasant dress looked like something Maddie's mother had worn when Maddie was a girl.

They made their way to the far side of the rink where Trish was lacing up ice skates. Zephyr, sporting a truly amazing Afro wig and a gold lamé jacket, balanced on his skates nearby.

"Where are your skates?" Trish asked when Maddie and Andrea reached her.

Andrea made a face. "I don't skate," she said.

"Why not?" Trish asked.

Andrea looked out at the ice rink. "Sliding around on that ice—it's too dangerous. I could fall and break something."

Trish snorted. "This from a woman who regularly hurtles down icy mountains."

"Skiing's different," Andrea said. She extended one booted leg. "Besides, these boots are part of my outfit."

"What about you?" Trish asked Maddie.

"If I take off these platform shoes, my pants drag on the ground," she said. "Not to mention these bell-bottoms are so wide I'm afraid they'd get caught in the skate blades." She looked around the packed building. "Who else is here that we know?"

"Max and Casey are out there somewhere. Heather and Ben. I saw Patti with some guy I'd never seen before." She finished lacing her skates and straightened. "I'll have to ask her about him."

"His name's Ryan," Zephyr said. "He's the new drummer with my band."

"What's the name of your band again?" Maddie asked.

"Moose Juice." He grinned. "We're playing a private party in Gunnison tomorrow night."

"Your fame is spreading beyond Crested Butte," Trish said drily.

Maddie wanted to ask if anyone had seen Hagan, but she was afraid they might take her interest the wrong way. She wasn't one of the groupies who panted after him. But she'd really enjoyed talking with him the few opportunities they'd had and she hadn't seen much of him lately at work.

The truth was, she'd missed him. He both aggravated and intrigued her. When she was with him, she thought less about her accident or her uncertain future, and more about, well, *Hagan*. Not that anything would come of those thoughts, or the zing of physical attraction she couldn't ignore when she was with him. But it gave her something to focus on besides her problems, and added an addictive spice to her days.

"That's the Way I Like It" began playing and Zephyr struck a disco pose, arms akimbo. "C'mon Trish, let's skate. This song rocks!"

Trish laughed, but skated onto the ice. They disappeared into the crowd.

"Let's get a drink," Andrea said.

They made their way to the bar. While they waited in line, Maddie had the sense someone was watching her. She turned and met a familiar pair of brilliant blue eyes.

"Hello, Maddie," Hagan said, coming over to stand beside her.

She told herself any man with a foreign accent would have made her feel all warm and gooshy inside, but why did she have to react that way to Hagan, of all people?

"Hi," she said, then forced her gaze away from his eyes. "That's some outfit you're wearing," she said, taking in the bright yellow one-piece ski suit. Made of some shiny wool/knit blend, with bell-bottom pants and wide lapels, it was a testament to the worst of seventies fashion.

"I saw Scott just now and he told me I look like a banana." He grinned. "A very tall banana."

"It says something about a man when he can wear something so hideous with confidence," she said. Mostly it said to her that Hagan could look good in anything.

The song ended and Trish and Zephyr joined them in line at the bar. "How is your shoulder?" Hagan asked Zephyr.

Zephyr frowned and shook his head, but Trish had already overheard them. "What happened to your shoulder?" she asked.

"Nothing." Zephyr dug his wallet from his pocket. "What do you want to drink? My treat."

"I'll buy my own drink," Trish said. "Don't change the subject." She looked at Hagan. "What did he do to his shoulder?"

Hagan shook his head. "You heard him—nothing."

She scowled at both of them. "I'll bet you two think you're being cute."

Just then Max, dressed in a mint-green leisure suit that was almost as hideous as Hagan's ski suit, and Casey, in an orange polyester minidress, joined them. "Hey." Max nodded to them. He turned to Zephyr. "Did Ben look at your shoulder? What did he say?"

"*What* is wrong with his shoulder?" Trish demanded.

"He made a bad landing over on Dead Bob this morning," Max said.

Trish frowned at Zephyr. "What is Dead Bob? Or do I want to know?"

"It's just the name of a run," Zephyr said. "It's no big deal. I'm fine."

"No, you're not," Trish said. "You're nuts." She glared at him, then turned away and headed for the ice. She skated across the rink and was soon swallowed up by the other partiers.

"What's up with her?" Max asked.

"She thinks the whole extreme skiing and boarding thing is nuts," Zephyr said.

"She looked pretty upset," Casey said.

"Sorry, dude," Max said. "I wouldn't have said anything if I'd known it was going to set her off."

"It's okay." Zephyr grinned. "Really."

"So you're glad Trish is upset with you?" Maddie said.

"Hey, it proves she cares, right?" He turned toward the bar. "But if you're feeling apologetic, Max, you can buy me a drink."

Max laughed. "Sure. And maybe I can figure out a way to make Trish really furious, since you like it so much."

"I think maybe he did land on his head too many times." Hagan's voice was low in Maddie's ear.

She glanced over her shoulder at him. "I don't know," she said. "I guess he figures dislike is better than indifference."

"Ah. That must be where I have gone wrong. I should expect a woman to dislike me first, before she could love me."

His tone was light, but his eyes held a sadness that made Maddie feel a little shaky. Was the playboy secretly longing for something more?

She was gathering the courage to ask him as much when he looked away. "It is very busy here tonight," he said. "I think I will leave early."

"You don't like crowds?" she asked, surprised. She'd imagined Hagan was a man who was always up for a party.

"Not tonight. Besides, this suit is not only ugly, it is uncomfortable." He nodded to her. "Good night. I will see you at work next week."

She stared after him as he slipped through the groups of people, a tall figure who drew the attention of almost everyone he passed, and not merely because of his outrageous attire. Tonight he radiated a certain tension, a restlessness that must have been contagious because Maddie felt it, too.

He'd mentioned love, a subject she couldn't recall ever hearing him broach before. Did watching Zephyr and Trish remind him of what was missing in his life, or had something else triggered his desire to leave the party?

"Where's Hagan going?" Max moved up beside her.

"He said it was too crowded in here. I guess he went home."

"That's not like Hagan," Casey said.

Max sipped his beer. "He's been in a weird mood lately."

"Where's Zephyr?" Maddie asked, uncomfortable about talking about Hagan anymore. She was afraid she'd say something to make people think he was more to her than another coworker. In her most private thoughts she could admit to a certain attraction to the man, but she never wanted anyone else to know she felt more than mild friendliness toward a man who'd set out to make himself so unreachable.

"He went to find Trish." Max laughed. "The guy never gives up."

"I think Trish has a soft spot for him," Casey said.

"No way," Max said. "Those two are too different. Trish is smart, successful, ambitious. And Zephyr is… Zephyr. In a class by himself."

"Some women like a man who presents a challenge," Casey said, looking at Max. Then she winked at Maddie. "Aren't you going to skate?"

"I don't think I can in these pants." Maddie looked down at the widely flared bell-bottoms.

"Sure you can," Max said. "Just roll up the legs." He tossed his empty cup in a nearby trash can. "Come on. This is Disco on Ice. You have to skate."

Casey joined in and Maddie allowed them to persuade her to roll up the cuffs of her pants and rent skates. To the sounds of Donna Summer, the Village People and other disco stars, she glided and twirled around the ice, discovering she hadn't forgotten the moves she'd known so well as a child.

"You're really good," Casey said when they stopped to take a break.

"I spent a lot of time on the ice when I was a kid," Maddie said. "Before I got serious about skiing."

"How old were you when you joined the U.S. ski team?" Casey asked.

"I made the junior team when I was fourteen," she

said. "Three years later, I joined the adult B team." She could still remember how elated she'd been the day she received her official racing uniform. She'd been sure then that nothing could stop her from achieving her dream of standing on the Olympic podium.

"It must have been hard, always training and traveling, not really having a normal high school and college life," Casey said.

"I didn't think of it as difficult," Maddie said. "I loved all of it, even the boring stuff like running and working out. It was all I ever wanted to do." She brushed a speck of glitter from someone else's costume off her thigh. "To tell you the truth, all the stuff you think of as normal feels odd to me. I've spent so many years focused on skiing, I sometimes don't know what to do with myself now."

"You could do anything," Casey said. "You could go to college, start a business, travel for pleasure, learn a new skill."

Except she didn't want to do any of those things. Her goal had been to ski, to be the best at that one thing she was good at. Now that it had been taken away from her, nothing held the same appeal. But how could anyone who hadn't been where she'd been, done what she'd done, understand that? "I just have to figure out what I want to do, I guess," she said with false cheerfulness. She hadn't managed to solve that puzzle in all the months since her injury, but maybe she was a slow learner. After all, she couldn't spend the rest of her life wishing things had worked out differently on that icy slope in St. Moritz.

Her thoughts turned to Hagan, and their conversation the other day on patrol. Something must have happened to make him leave his corporate job for a very different life here in Crested Butte. If she knew more of his story, maybe she'd gain some insight into her own dilemma. Had Hagan, like her, retreated from some mistake or tragedy? Or was he the rare person who had decided what he wanted to do with his life and done it?

But if a life of seasonal jobs and brief affairs was the perfect one for Hagan, he didn't look too happy lately. According to his friends, it wasn't usual for him to leave a party early, yet he'd stayed around less than an hour tonight.

Speaking of leaving, she checked her watch. It was after midnight, and she had to work tomorrow. She said goodbye to the others and left while Zephyr was trying to prove he could spin on ice skates while the others egged him on.

Self-conscious about riding the bus in her costume, Maddie had driven her car. As she turned down the street toward her condo, she was surprised to see a familiar truck parked outside the grocery/liquor store/ coffee shop on the corner. She slowed and checked again. Yes, that was definitely Hagan's truck. She recognized the Nordic flag sticker on the bumper.

On impulse, she pulled into the lot and parked beside him. Whatever had driven Hagan to leave the party early, he hadn't gone home.

He was easy enough to spot in the small shop, even without the bright yellow ski suit. He sat at a table in the corner, a Denver paper spread around him, a large cup of coffee in front of him. "Hello, Hagan," she said as she slipped into the chair across from him.

He looked up and frowned at her. "Hello, Maddie. What are you doing here?"

"I was going to ask you the same thing."

"I decided I wanted coffee."

Two hours was a long time to sit drinking coffee and reading the paper, but maybe he hadn't been here the whole time. Maybe he'd met up with one of his girlfriends and was only now on his way home.

To hide her discomfort, she picked up a section of the paper. "Anything interesting in here?"

"Not really." He set aside the paper and turned his attention to her. "How was the party?"

"It was fun. How come you didn't stick around?"

He shrugged, but offered no further answer.

So he was in one of those moods, was he? The strong, silent type might appeal to some women but Maddie preferred a man who talked to her. Not that she had any intention of Hagan being her man, but she would keep firing questions at him until they had a real conversation or he walked out.

First, she got up and ordered a decaf latte. When she returned to the table, he was still there. She took this as a small sign of encouragement and made herself comfortable. "Where *did* you get that outfit?" she asked.

"A thrift store in Gunnison. It was marked down to five dollars."

"I wonder why." She grinned and thought she detected a twitch at the corners of his mouth.

"Where did you get yours?" His gaze swept over her costume, lingering at the scant cleavage displayed at the neck of her blouse.

Heat spread through her in response to that look. If

he could do this to her with a look, imagine what would happen if he ever actually kissed her…. She shifted in her chair and tried to push the thought away. "Probably the same thrift shop," she said. "To tell you the truth, I kind of like it." She stirred sweetener into her coffee. "But then, after those form-fitting racing suits I spent so much time in, almost anything looks good." She made a face. "Put a racing uni on any woman and she looks like she ought to have a wide load warning on her backside."

"Some men appreciate that particular feature of a woman's anatomy."

Yes, he was definitely smiling now. Almost. Another warm flush swept over her. She'd heard this observation before, but hearing it again from Hagan—a man whose dates always resembled dancers in music videos—pleased her.

"I remember when people wore ski suits like that," she said, nodding to his outfit. "I think my dad had a similar one in red."

He nodded. "They were never the fashion in Norway, but I have seen pictures."

"I've been to Norway a couple of times," she said. "To Kvitfjell to watch a men's race, and to Lillehammer, where they held the 1994 Olympics. It's a beautiful country."

He nodded. "It is."

This was his cue to elaborate on his childhood in Norway, or some favorite thing about his homeland. Was he homesick? Did he ever go back? But he showed no inclination to play the game.

She wondered if tossing her coffee in his lap would

liven things up any, but decided that would be a little extreme. Not to mention immature and messy. The thing was, she didn't sense that Hagan was actually being rude—he was simply a man who liked silence.

Fine. She could do silence when she had to. She picked the sports section from the pile of newspapers and scanned its pages. An article about hockey on the front page. Basketball. Baseball training camp. Golf.

Boring, boring, boring.

On the inside back page a photo at the top caught her eye. A woman in a U.S.A. ski uni stood atop a podium, a bouquet of flowers in her arms, a medal around her neck. Maddie peered closer and her stomach began to hurt as she read.

"What is wrong?" Hagan asked.

"What makes you think something's wrong?" She pushed the paper aside, though her gaze kept darting back to the picture.

"Your face went white just now. Did you read something that upset you?"

The man might not say much, but she had to give him points for being observant. Maybe too observant. "A teammate of mine won the World Cup title in women's downhill." She looked at the picture again. "She was on the B team when I was on the A team."

"And now she is where you wanted to be."

Ouch. No beating around the bush for him. "Yeah." She picked up the paper and read. "Julia Manchester has risen rapidly through the ranks of women skiers. She's being compared to former U.S. stars Picabo Street and Maddie Alexander."

Even Hagan had the grace to wince. They were both

silent for a moment, then he said, "It is a strange feeling when a reminder from the past pops up like that. Something to recall where we ourselves might be if things had been different."

She wondered again at the man's understanding. Maybe it was because he spent more time thinking than talking. She gave him a grateful look. "I think that's it. If things had worked out differently, that would be me on that podium now." If she hadn't been so stubborn... so stupid.

He nodded, and picked up another section of the paper. "Before you came in, I was reading about a man I knew years ago. We worked together. David Moreland." He tapped the paper. "He has his own company now and is very successful."

She leaned forward to get a better look at the article—something about a company called Moreland Solutions. "What kind of work did you do together?"

"Computers. I wrote software."

She blinked, trying to wrap her mind around this idea. Hagan had the thoughtful, deliberate manner she suspected was required to create complicated computer code, but he definitely didn't fit her picture of the typical programmer. "You were a geek?"

The word at last brought a smile to his lips. "Yes. I was a geek." He glanced at the paper. "And now my old friend is a very wealthy geek."

"Does that make you wish you had done things differently?"

He shook his head. "No. I am not one to look back. I made the choices I made and am happy with them. I think the shock is more that I had not thought of that life in a very long time. I forget sometimes I even lived that way."

"I wish I could say the same," she said. "But I'm not there yet. I look at this picture and all I feel is envy." She looked at him, searching his eyes for answers. "Is there a secret?" she asked. "To having no regrets?"

He shook his head. "I do not know. Maybe it is a matter of time."

She sighed. "That's what they told me when I was in the hospital. In time, I'd feel better. In time I'd forget all about wanting what I couldn't have."

"It will get better," he said. "You are young and healthy and too smart to live in the past." He stood and shrugged into his jacket. "We both have to work tomorrow. We should go."

"Yes." She was reluctant to end the evening, wanting to hang on to the closeness she felt to him. But she put on her coat and followed him out to the parking lot. She lingered by his truck, wondering if this would be the night he did more than walk away from her. The night he would kiss her, and admit that he, too, felt the physical pull between them.

But he climbed into his truck without looking at her again, except for a casual wave goodbye as he started the engine. She watched as he drove away, longing for the courage to make the first move with Hagan, but fearing she'd destroy their tentative friendship if she pushed him too far, too fast. Better she keep her secret fantasies to herself.

Hagan had given her a lot to think about tonight— not so much with his words, but with what she'd seen in his eyes during those last moments they'd looked at each other. There was something he wasn't saying. She believed him when he said he didn't feel regret, but there was pain there nonetheless. A pain that didn't look that different than what she herself was feeling.

Chapter Seven

When there wasn't an official reason to throw a party, Maddie's new friends would make their own. A week after the Winter Carnival, Maddie had already changed into her pajamas one evening when Andrea burst into the condo and started dragging ski gear out of the front closet. "A bunch of us are going for a moonlight ski up on Kebler Pass," she said. "You've got to come. Where is my avi beacon?"

"Top shelf, next to mine." Maddie pointed to the GameBoy-size avalanche beacon. The beacon would either send a signal to lead searchers to the wearer buried in an avalanche or would allow the wearer to detect a buried skier who also wore a beacon. "So this is in the backcountry?" she asked, watching Andrea haul out a backpack, water bottles, telemark skis and a heavy-duty parka.

"Yes. Great powder and awesome scenery." She looked back over her shoulder at Maddie. "It's a full moon tonight. We're all going to bring food and drinks and everything. You should come."

The thought of skiing untracked powder beneath the

light of a full moon was too much to resist. Maddie dove into the closet beside Andrea and began hauling out her own gear.

Half an hour later in Andrea's Subaru, they followed a line of vehicles up the winding road to Kebler Pass. They found a spot in the parking area, climbed out and began unloading their gear. "What did you girls bring to eat?" Zephyr asked as he unlocked the ski rack atop his Jeep, which he'd parked next to them.

"Peanut butter and banana sandwiches, and a thermos of cocoa spiked with peppermint schnapps," Andrea said.

"Awesome," he said. "Trish brought brownies from her coffee shop and I packed leftover pizza."

"Pizza?" Andrea made a face. "Isn't that messy to carry?"

"Nah. You're gonna smush it all together when you eat it anyway." He lifted a snowboard out of the rack. "Everything tastes great up here after a run anyway."

Two big dogs, each with their own avalanche beacon, raced among the cars. "Whose dogs?" Maddie asked.

"The golden one is Molly. She belongs to Max. The black one is Lucy. She's Molly's daughter and lives with Casey."

Maddie nodded. She'd about figured out the people who went together; she guessed dogs were the next step. Though she still had a few questions about the humans—were Trish and Zephyr a couple, or merely friends? And who was Hagan with tonight?

She found herself searching for the tall Norseman and spotted him with Max and Casey at the other end of the parking lot. When he looked her way, she ducked her head and pretended to be adjusting her gloves.

Neither had mentioned their conversation at the coffee shop after the Disco on Ice party. Confidences like that, shared late at night, were harder to acknowledge in the light of every day. In some ways, Maddie felt privileged to have had this glimpse of Hagan's more serious side, but she also wondered how wise she'd been to confide in him. She wasn't proud of her jealousy over her former teammate's win, or her inability to let go of her own self-pity over all she'd lost. Sharing these feelings with a man who went out of his way to avoid getting too close to people made her wonder if she was reading more into her casual friendship with Hagan than was warranted.

She had to figure out her future for herself, and not make the mistake of relying on a man who appeared to have given up on anything that smacked of ambition or permanence.

Eight of them had gathered to make the run: Hagan, Max, Zephyr and his friend Bryan, Andrea, Trish, Casey and Maddie. Bryan passed around a flask of cinnamon schnapps and they each took a sip, the sweet, peppery liqueur radiating warmth through Maddie's chest. The moon bathed the landscape in silvery light, turning the world into a black-and-white photo full of sharp contrasts, dark trees making slashes of shadow against white snow. Their breath froze in front of them and frost formed on their eyebrows, on Max's goatee and on the ends of Zephyr's dreadlocks. They spoke in hushed tones, their laughter subdued, instinctively not wanting to disturb the eerie peace of the night. There was a magic in an experience like this. In all the years she'd skied, she'd never done so under the light of the full moon.

The snow squeaked beneath their feet as they gathered at the start of a trail leading up above the parking lot. In single file, they made their way up the trail. The snowboarders had to shoulder their boards and climb. Most of the skiers had climbing skins—thin chamois strips that attached to the bottom of their skis and helped provide traction.

For a long time, the only sounds were the squeak of boots on snow and the huff of their breath as the trail grew steeper. Even in such beautiful surroundings, climbing up was hard work. By the time they neared the top even the fittest of them was panting and groaning. "Come on people, you have to earn your turns," Max chided. "That's what makes it worthwhile."

They spread out along the trail and strapped on snowboards or removed climbing skins and adjusted bindings on skis. Maddie found herself next to Hagan. He was a tall, lean figure all in black, even the brightness of his hair hidden by a black helmet. "There are many lines you can ski from here," he said. "After a while the terrain levels out and you must hike back up."

She nodded. "Thanks." With so many people and such good light, she felt confident she could find her way around. And even though they all wore beacons, the chance of an avalanche seemed low.

Max and Zephyr took off first, and the others soon followed, dropping off the packed trail into deep, soft powder. Maddie let out a yelp of delight as she sailed through her first turn, her skis disappearing in the thick fluff. She felt as if she was floating in a sea of snow, curving around stands of trees, flying down narrower chutes. She could hear the others around her, whooping and shouting, and from time to time she would glimpse a dark figure ahead of her or to one side in the trees.

She felt as if she'd been initiated into a special club, kindred spirits who appreciated the magic of skiing and the beauty of the moonlit night. Here, on this back-country slope, she felt more at home than she had since moving to town.

Too soon, the terrain flattened and the revelers made their way back to the parking lot, where they stopped to drink hot cocoa and tea and share the food they'd brought. They spread the contents of their backpacks on the hood of Max's Jeep and helped themselves to this eclectic buffet. Maddie discovered that leftover smushed pizza, hummus on crackers and peanut butter and banana sandwiches all tasted wonderful in the cold, crisp air.

The *very* cold air. Temperatures must have been well below zero. In her layers of clothing and thick parka, she was warm everywhere except her hands. "I should have worn mittens instead of these gloves," she said to Andrea, tucking her hands beneath her armpits to try and warm them.

"Too bad we didn't think to bring firewood," Andrea said. "We could have built a fire."

"I have some chemical handwarmers in my pack," Casey volunteered. "You can have a pair if you like."

"You'll warm up when you start climbing again," Max said.

"Thanks," Maddie said to Casey. "But Max is right. I'll be fine." And next time, she'd remember to wear mittens.

Hunger sated, they began the hike again. Energized

by the previous run, they talked and laughed and teased each other. At a wider spot on the trail, Hagan shuffled alongside Maddie. "Are you as fast in this powder as you are on a race course?" he asked.

"Not *as* fast," she said. "But fast." She grinned. "Do you want to race?"

"It hardly seems fair," he said. "I have much longer legs than you."

"But I have better moves."

He smiled—a genuine, full-on smile, not one of the half-serious almost-smirks that passed for a smile from him most of the time. "Then we will race."

She felt a surge of adrenaline at the challenge. Sure, it was only an amateur challenge among friends, but the chance to experience the rush of speed and competition again, even in this small way, invigorated her. She attacked the uphill climb with renewed energy. As the trail narrowed, Hagan fell in behind her, and she was aware of him on her heels the rest of the way up.

At the top she removed her climbing skins, adjusted her boots, then gripped her poles and poised at the edge of a dropoff. "Are you ready?" she asked him.

"I'm read—"

She didn't wait to hear more, but dove off the trail.

She heard laughter behind her and felt him on her heels, but she went into a tighter tuck and pointed her skis downhill. These were not good racing conditions—the powder was too thick, and there were too many trees. Real race courses were groomed to the consistency of ice, and free of obstacles that weren't man-made. But the same sensation of flying and freedom filled her as she swung hard around trees and tucked for the straightaway.

Best of all, there was no fear here. The powder kept her speed down and if she fell in this fluff it would be like falling in a featherbed. She could abandon herself to the pure joy of speed and snow.

She reached the flat almost too soon and skidded to a halt, turning to taunt Hagan as he came in behind her. But he wasn't there.

She stared up the slope, noticing that hers were the only tracks. There should have been some remnants from their earlier run that night. She waited longer, listening for the sounds of others, but heard nothing—no shouting, no voices—nothing but the creak of tree branches rubbing together in a gust of wind.

She looked around, hoping to spot some landmark from her earlier run, but nothing looked familiar, especially in this silver-and-shadow world. She began to shiver, the icy wind cutting through the layers of fleece and wool she wore. And now that she was stopped, her hands were freezing again. Her fingertips ached with the cold. She shoved her hands deep into the pockets of her parka and wished she'd taken Casey up on her offer of the chemical handwarmers. The little packages of iron oxide would have helped a lot.

Okay. She took a deep breath, trying to remember all her emergency response training. She'd started at the top; the thing to do was to climb back up. She must have skied over the road—perhaps beyond the parking area, where it was snowpacked and closed. If she headed toward the top of the pass, she'd find the road eventually and could make her way back to the others.

With a heavy sigh, she planted her pole and began climbing.

It was hard going, the slope steeper than she remembered. She was tired and cold and the water bladder in her pack was almost empty. And she could no longer feel her fingers.

This is ridiculous, she grumbled. She stopped and pulled her cell phone from her pack, thinking she'd call Andrea and see if they could figure out where she was. But the screen showed no signal—not that unusual in a land of mountains, tall trees, and few people or cell phone towers.

She had emergency gear in her pack, including a whistle. She could blow the standard distress signal— three short puffs in succession—and likely someone would hear her and find her.

She shook her head and began climbing again. She'd only do that as a last resort. She would never hear the end of it if she got lost. The story would spread through the whole patrol. Worse, she'd deserve the ridicule they'd heap on her. She'd been showing off, trying to beat Hagan, and she hadn't had the sense to pay attention to where she was going.

She climbed steadily, pausing every few yards to rest and listen for the others. But all she heard was her own harsh breathing and the wind, which had increased in intensity. It felt colder now, too, in spite of the exertion of the climb.

She was doing fine, making her way steadily uphill, until she came to a thick stand of trees, spindly trunked firs crowded together too close to squeeze through. She started left, trying to make her way around them, and encountered a deep ravine. Right was more trees. She looked around, confused. How had she ended up here? She'd come down, so there had to be a way back up.

But she could see none. And going down went against everything she'd been taught in her training. Down could be a bottomless canyon, a riverbed or sheer cliffs.

She stared at the landscape of black trees and white snow, then dug in her pack and pulled out the whistle. Raising it to her lips, she blew three short, sharp blasts, all the while doing her best not to cry.

HALFWAY DOWN THE RUN, Hagan lost sight of Maddie in the trees. She was indeed faster than him, and her smaller size gave her an advantage in the narrow chutes and tightly spaced trees. He was sorry he was not able to catch up with her, but would concede defeat graciously when they met up again.

Maybe it was just as well she had outpaced him. He could do with some time alone to cool off. Following her up the trail, he had had the enticing view of her curvy backside for the better part of a half hour. The sight had made it impossible for him to focus on anything else. He was definitely aroused, almost oblivious to the arduous climb as his mind conjured erotic fantasies involving a naked Maddie, a very large bed, and the time to explore each other properly. He had proposed the race as a physical outlet and a distraction.

Of all the women who had practically thrown themselves at him, why would this one—who had at times seemed to barely tolerate his presence—be the one to catch him off guard? She was as different from the pretty flirts and sexy sirens he usually dated as he could imagine.

Which was part of the problem. He gravitated to easy, uncomplicated women because they posed no danger of engaging deeper emotions. A woman like Maddie, one who aroused not only his physical passion, but his curiosity and his protective instincts, was definitely dangerous to his well-being.

He had felt the danger there in the coffee shop, when he had told her about his past as a software writer. He had revealed more about himself to Maddie than he had told anyone for years. He told himself he had done it to comfort her. She had obviously been upset at learning her former competition had achieved a goal Maddie had long sought. He had understood that feeling and wanted her to know she was not alone.

But such confidences made him feel too vulnerable and he had forced himself to pull back. He liked Maddie and valued her friendship, but he could not afford to take things further. He did not want to venture into the messy territory of more intimate relationships, where the fallout from a single misstep or misjudgment was too much to bear.

He took his time making his way to the parking area, where the others were packing up and preparing to leave. He stopped beside his truck and began to take off his own skis when Andrea approached him. "Where's Maddie?" she asked.

He looked around and realized Maddie was not in the group gathered around the cars. "She was ahead of me," he said. "I thought she was already back."

Andrea looked worried. "She's not here. And the last time I saw her, she was with you."

He took his skis from the rack and clicked into the bindings once more, his voice calm, though his heart was pounding. "We had better look for her." Even someone who was familiar with the area could get lost in the backcountry. She could ski into a box canyon, or an area of cliffs. She could fall and break a bone, or get trapped in a tree well. His stomach twisted as his mind catalogued the possibilities. He never should have let her ski off by herself that way.

Andrea alerted the others and they soon gathered around Hagan. He supposed as the most experienced in backcountry rescue, both as a patroller and with the local search and rescue squad, they looked to him as a leader.

"Zephyr, you and Bryan stay here with the vehicles in case she returns," he said. The two snowboarders would have a more difficult time in the varying terrain they would need to cover. "Do you have whistles?"

"I have one," Bryan said.

"Me, too," Zephyr added.

"Signal if she shows up." Though in the vast terrain, with all the sound-absorbing snow and trees, it was possible a whistle might not be heard. "If no one responds to the whistle, honk one of the car horns."

"If that doesn't work, I can plug in my guitar and turn the amp up loud," Zephyr said.

"We want an emergency signal, not an avalanche trigger," Max said.

The searchers set out: Max and Casey with the dogs, Trish with Andrea, and Hagan by himself.

"Maybe you should come with us," Andrea said. "It would probably be safer."

"I will be all right on my own."

She looked up at him, her face drawn with worry. "Do you think she's all right? I mean, she's had back-country rescue training, right?"

"She has not been gone that long," Hagan said. "She will be fine." But he knew things could turn bad very quickly out here. The backcountry was a fun place to play, but the isolated terrain, below-freezing temperatures and natural hazards could also be deadly.

He headed toward the area where he had last seen Maddie ski into the trees. He moved quickly, forcing himself to make note of landmarks, to maintain an awareness of his surroundings. The last thing they needed was for him to lose his way also. He silently inventoried the emergency supplies in his pack: extra food and water, first-aid supplies, matches and firestarters, whistle and signaling mirror, compass, knife, maps, space blanket. Was Maddie as well-prepared? Even if she was, none of it would make any difference if she was injured.

He forced the thought out of his mind. She was an experienced skier and not the type to panic. She would be all right.

It was after two in the morning and by all rights he should have been exhausted, but adrenaline and nerves lent strength to his muscles. He moved forward with strong, sure strides, until he came to the area where he was sure Maddie had raced ahead of him out of sight.

The moon was still bright, and he studied the snow, searching for a single set of tracks heading away from all the others. He found twin lines in the drifts of powder heading downhill and followed them, growing increasingly worried as he advanced. If these tracks were Maddie's, she was heading away from the parking area, toward a ravine choked with trees.

He forced himself to stop and catch his breath, and drink some water. On a hunch, he pulled out his whistle and blew a sharp blast on it, then listened for a response.

Was it his imagination, or did he hear a faint reply? Was that the wind or three blasts from another whistle? Maddie? Or one of the other searchers?

He blew again, and his heart raced as the reply came again, stronger this time. Moving as quickly as he dared, he skied toward the sound, pausing every hundred yards or so to blow his own whistle and wait for the response.

She was in such a dense stand of trees, he did not see her at first. Then he spotted movement and suddenly he recognized her. She was waving both arms at him, and shouting his name.

"Hagan! Thank God you've come." She skied to him and practically fell into his arms.

Chapter Eight

Hagan held Maddie close, waiting for his heartbeat to slow before he trusted himself to speak. His relief at finding her was like a balloon expanding in his lungs, stealing his breath and leaving him weak. She laid her head on his chest, her arms around him, her shoulders shaking—from cold or from tears?

He pulled back far enough to lift her chin. Ice streaked her cheeks where she had been crying. "Shh," he said. "It is all right now. Are you hurt?"

She shook her head. "Only my pride. I can't believe I was so stupid."

"What happened?" he asked.

"I don't know. One minute I was skiing, the next I had no idea where I was. I kept trying to find my way back up to where I started, but I only got more turned around. Then I got into these trees and couldn't see a way out."

"We will follow my tracks back out. Are you sure you are all right?"

"Just cold." She hugged her arms around her body. "Especially my hands. I can't feel my fingers."

"Let me see."

Reluctantly, she let him take her hands. He stripped off one of her gloves and studied her fingers. They were very white and the skin was hard, almost waxy. "You have frostbite," he said. "We must warm your fingers right away."

"I've been putting them in my pockets as much as I can," she said. "But it's freezing."

"How are your feet?" he asked. Extremities were the first to freeze.

"I have boot heaters." She indicated the battery-operated heaters attached to her boots. "I remembered those, it's my mittens I forgot."

"We have to get your hands to normal temperature." He let go of her and unzipped his jacket and began pulling up the fleece shirt and long underwear top he wore.

"What are you doing?" she asked, eyes widening in alarm.

"Put your hands on my stomach," he said. "My body heat will help you."

She shook her head. "Hagan, my hands are too cold, I—"

"Do it." He grabbed her wrists and forced her hands beneath his shirt.

Her skin was like ice, and he sucked in a sharp breath, but refused to allow her to pull away. After a few seconds, she relaxed, and spread her fingers wide, shaping them to his abdomen.

As the first shock of cold subsided, he was aware of her touching him, of the smallness of her hands, the softness of her skin. The intimacy of their position moved him—not only the physical closeness, but the emotional vulnerability he felt, as if he had bared more than his skin to her. He was used to adopting a certain distance with people, even his lovers. But Maddie breached his reserves and touched parts of him he had kept carefully hidden away for years. The knowledge troubled him, and yet he found himself wanting to be with her more and more, like an adrenaline junkie drawn to danger.

She stood with her head bent, not looking at him, but he was aware of her breathing, shallow and rapid like his own. She wore a blue knit hat with a large pom-pom on top, and he could just see the curve of her cheek, a lock of her brown hair curling against it. It took everything in him not to pull her to him, to hold her and kiss her and confess how afraid he had been that she had come to some harm.

And beyond that relief were deeper feelings of longing and desire. As they stood in that intimate embrace, surrounded by moon-washed darkness, his earlier arousal returned stronger than ever. Standing so close, she had to be aware of his physical response to her. Was she appalled or angry?

Or was it possible she wanted him also?

The idea shook him. He did not want to be this caught up with anyone, to feel so close to losing the careful control he had perfected all these years. For ten years, he had been the one in charge of whatever relationship he was in. With Maddie he felt as if he was no longer calling the shots—as if some force outside himself was compelling him to seek her out, pushing aside reason and caution in favor of his need to be with her.

"I—I think my fingers are thawed now," she said. But she made no move to pull away.

He kept one hand on her shoulder, but wrapped the other around her fingers. They were warmer now. "How do they feel?" he asked.

She grimaced. "They hurt. A lot."

He nodded. "That is a good sign. It means the nerves are not damaged."

She slipped from his grasp then, and looked at her reddened fingers. "I guess I'd better have my gloves back." Still she did not look at him. Just as well. He did not know how well he could keep his own feelings from showing in his eyes.

She put on her gloves while he zipped his jacket. "Can you follow me out of here?" he asked.

She nodded. "If the alternative is being left behind, I think I could do anything."

"Let us go. When we get up a little closer to the road I will try signaling to the others."

She looked dismayed. "Is everyone out searching for me?"

"Most of them. Zephyr and Bryan are waiting at the parking area, in case you returned there."

"How humiliating," she moaned. "They'll never let me hear the end of this."

"Anyone can get lost out here," he said. "It is one of the realities of the backcountry. Even experts have accidents. People who teach avalanche courses have died in avalanches. People go out for one hour, the weather changes and they get off course and we find them three days later. Everyone who lives here knows these things. No one will think less of you for this."

The smile she gave him was an arrow to his heart. "Thank you," she said. "For saying that. And for finding me. For warming my fingers and…and for everything."

Her eyes shone with such admiration and true affection, he had to look away. That, or pull her to him and kiss her until they both were breathless. Instead, he turned and started out of the bunched trees. "Follow me," he said. "This will all be over soon."

MADDIE WELCOMED the hard work of making the climb back up the slope. It warmed her body and forced her to concentrate on something besides the man ahead of her. Back there in the trees, warming her hands beneath Hagan's shirt, desire had hit her with the force of an avalanche. She'd felt his pulse beneath her fingers, and the ridged line of muscle along his abdomen and had to lock her knees to stay upright.

Along with physical desire came a feeling of profound connection to the man before her. When he'd held her so tightly after he'd first found her, she'd felt so safe. So comforted. And when she'd looked into his eyes she knew that he understood her—her fears and flaws and silly weaknesses—in a way that maybe no one else ever had. The certainty of this knowledge and her powerful physical attraction to him caught her off guard.

On the heels of this came the realization that she was not alone in her response to the situation. Hagan was aroused, as well. Was it only the situation that caused this unexpected intimacy in the moonlit darkness? Or was it *her* he wanted?

At the top of the ridge, they stopped to rest and

Hagan blew a long sharp blast on his whistle. "I hope everyone hears that and comes in," she said. "I hate to think of them out in this cold."

"They will be glad to know you are all right," he said. He hesitated, then added, "I should have never let you ski off alone that way. I knew you were unfamiliar with the area."

"It's not your fault," she protested. "I was the one who wasn't paying attention to where I was going."

"I feel responsible. When I returned to the parking lot and you were not there…" He shook his head, his expression grim. "I have never felt so sick at heart."

His evident distress moved her. She reached out and squeezed his arm. "It's okay. You found me and I'm fine." She wanted to say more, but she couldn't find words for all she was feeling. And given his penchant for avoiding emotional entanglements, maybe that was just as well. She'd come to value his friendship; no sense ruining that with deeper feelings that would only make him retreat.

He nodded and stashed the whistle in his pocket. "Let's go. The others will be waiting."

Zephyr and Bryan ran to meet them as they emerged from the trees into the parking area. "Way to go, Hagan!" Zephyr said. "Where was she?"

"I got turned around in a bunch of trees," Maddie said, trying to make light of the situation.

"Hey, Maddie! Are you all right?" Andrea clicked out of her skis and ran to meet them. She threw her arms around Maddie, almost knocking her over.

"I'm fine," Maddie said, laughing.

"We were so worried," Andrea said.

"Hagan, did you find her?" Max and Casey joined the group and Max slapped Hagan on the back.

"I was probably the last to see her, so I had a good idea where to start looking," he said. "She was smart enough to stay in one place and wait for someone to come along."

Not smart. Terrified, she thought, but didn't correct him.

"I think maybe Hagan just wanted an excuse to get you off by himself," Max said, ignoring Hagan's scowl.

"I'd have been a basket case, out there in the dark by myself," Casey said, hugging Maddie.

"I'm glad you're okay, Maddie," Bryan said.

"Me, too," Zephyr said. "We were all worried about you."

Somehow, in the weeks since she'd arrived in Crested Butte, alone and feeling so isolated, she had become one of them—part of this family of friends who cared about one another. The competitive racing world didn't foster this kind of closeness, and she wasn't sure yet how to handle it. But their genuine concern touched her more than she could find the words to express. "Thanks, everybody," she said.

"Are you sure you're okay?" Casey asked.

"I'm fine." She stifled a yawn. "Just tired."

"We all are," Hagan said. "Let us go home."

With the heater in Andrea's car going full blast, she and Maddie joined the caravan down the pass. "I'll bet you were really glad to see Hagan when he showed up," Andrea said.

"I was." She would have been grateful for anyone coming to her rescue, but Hagan had not only rescued her, he had salvaged her bruised ego. In so many ways he was different from her, not only because he was a man and she was a woman, but because they had entirely different outlooks on life. He kept his emotions hidden, while she wore hers close to the surface. He avoided intimacy at all costs while she welcomed the newfound closeness to others that her career had previously made difficult to find.

Despite these difference, in those minutes when she had stood with her hands on his stomach she'd fallen a little in love with him. She hadn't meant for it to happen—hadn't wanted it to happen—but it had been as inevitable as the sunrise.

There was nothing she could do about it, of course. Hagan had made it clear there was no room in his life for long-term love. Her feelings for him would have to be her secret. Something she would consider with longing and regret.

One more dream that would never come true.

HEATHER AND BEN were married on Valentine's Day at the Crested Butte Country Club. The weather cooperated, the brilliant sunshine bleaching the snow to the white of clouds, and temperatures climbing into the forties.

Hagan stood with Max at Ben's side, fighting the urge to tug at the collar of his tuxedo. He felt as if he was choking, and not only because of the tightness of the collar. Weddings made him uneasy; it was like watching people dancing on the edge of a chasm. He wanted to warn them to be careful, but everyone was in such a happy mood, he knew they would not listen.

Not that every marriage ended badly. Plenty of people stayed together and even seemed happy. But there was no way of predicting who would be lucky enough to know nothing but sweetness and light, and who would one day wake up with the bitter taste of betrayal.

And then he felt guilty for even thinking such thoughts about his friends. The two of them deserved every bit of their happiness. Ben could not stop grinning, for all his hand shook when Max handed him the ring for Heather's finger. Heather herself radiated joy, her eyes shining with happy tears as she looked into Ben's eyes and said her vows.

Hagan was glad these two had found each other—glad because he thought they suited each other, and glad that he no longer had to worry about Heather mooning after him. When she had set her cap for him he had been reluctant to speak to her or even look at her too long for fear she would take it as encouragement. Things were much easier now that the two of them could be friends. And maybe she and Ben would be among the lucky ones for whom marriage was the beginning of a good life together.

The ceremony concluded, the wedding party made their way to the ballroom for the reception. Hagan *did* loosen his tie then, and headed straight for the bar for a fortifying drink. He was waiting his turn in line when Maddie joined him. She was wearing a blue dress of some slinky material, with thin straps that showed off her toned arms and shoulders. She looked…feminine. Desirable.

He had to turn away for a moment to rein in his

emotions. This instant *physical* response to her confused him. He appreciated beautiful women, had dated more than his share of them, but none had made him feel this…this out of control. And why Maddie? Why now? They were friends. Coworkers. How could something as simple as seeing her in a dress affect him this way?

Then again, maybe it was not the dress, but what had happened between them that night on the mountain. A line had been crossed there in the darkness, the line between coworkers and friends and something more intense. More intimate. Somehow, Maddie had touched more than his bare skin in those few moments.

"I see all the single people made a beeline for the bar," she said.

Hagan had no way of knowing if all the people in line at the bar were really single, but certainly many of the ones he recognized were unattached. "Why do you say that?" he asked.

"It's awkward, being single at a wedding," she said. "The whole *point* of a wedding is to celebrate two people pairing off, so if you're not already part of a pair it feels…uncomfortable." She looked around the room, which was fast filling up with guests. Near the bar, a DJ was setting up. Hagan noticed Maddie was wearing silver earrings with little blue stones strung on thin wires that hung almost to her shoulders. They caught his eye every time she moved her head, drawing his attention to the long line of her neck. He found himself wondering what it would be like to kiss her there….

"Whenever I'm at these things I never know whether to feel relieved that I'm not in the bride's shoes or sad that my life is lacking something because I'm not part of a twosome," she said.

He jerked his gaze away from her and stepped up to the bar. "You could have brought a date," he said. He ordered a beer. "What would you like?" he asked her.

"White wine, please. Thanks." She accepted the glass of wine, then said, "Bringing a date to a wedding is worse. Too much pressure." She looked him in the eye. "Tell me the truth now. Have you ever attended a wedding with a woman and *not* wondered if she was trying to send you a hint about where she expected your relationship to lead?"

He had avoided weddings for the past ten years, but he understood her point. "When you attend a wedding with a man, are you silently contemplating how he would look in a tux standing beside you in a white gown?"

She laughed. "No. I'm too busy worrying he'll think I'm pressuring him into something neither one of us want." They walked away from the bar to a spot on the edge of the dance floor and watched Ben lead Heather out for the first dance.

"Do you go to a lot of weddings?" he asked.

"I have six female cousins, all near my age, and all married. For a few years there it seemed as if I spent every summer going from one wedding to another. I kept hoping one of them would decide to get married during ski season, so I'd have a good excuse to bow out, but no such luck." She sipped her wine. "The only reason I've ever brought a date to a wedding was to keep all my female relatives, older friends and general busybodies from trying to fix me up with any single men at the reception."

"You were not worried about that today?"

She shook her head. "My relatives aren't here and I *think* I'm still new enough in town to be safe from the general busybodies. Besides, the whole date thing is complicated. In addition to worrying he'll think I've set him up, there are always other guests—usually women, I'll admit—who see an unengaged or unmarried couple and feel compelled to impress upon them all the joys and benefits of being married, and don't *they* want to have a celebration like this one day soon?"

"I think I am glad I have not attended any of the weddings you have," he said.

She gave him a long look. Did he imagine the flare of heat in her eyes, or was it only because of his own heightened temperature?

"You've probably avoided the hard sell because you're a man." She smiled. "Besides, you're handsome enough even the old biddies are too busy flirting with you to worry about pairing you up with some hapless spinster."

He almost choked on his beer, both at the use of the old-fashioned word and at the idea of old *biddies* flirting with him. Yes, he was accustomed to the attention of women; he had been aware from an early age there was something in him that attracted the opposite sex, and he had used this to his advantage on numerous occasions. But it was not something he consciously worked at all the time. It was part of who he was, like his blond hair or his height, but he resented that so many people never saw past this surface.

Ben ended his dance with Heather by bending her backward and kissing her passionately. The crowd applauded, and other couples joined the newlyweds on the dance floor as a new song began. Maddie swayed in time to the music. Hagan had the sense she was not even aware she was doing it.

One of the men who had served as an usher during the ceremony, a doctor friend of Ben's, approached them. "Would you like to dance?" he asked Maddie.

The thought of her in another man's arms, even for the duration of a dance, was too much for Hagan. He took her elbow and said, "She was just about to dance with me."

WITH ALMOST ANY OTHER MAN, Maddie would have pulled away and reminded him she was capable of making up her own mind who to dance with. But she wouldn't pass up this chance to be physically close to Hagan, even in the context of a dance in a room full of people.

She had struggled to put all thought of the moonlit night when he had rescued her out of her mind, to erase the memory of his arms around her, her fingers pressed against the heat of his abdomen, his pulse pounding as wildly as her own heart.

At work, she had managed to hide her feelings, focusing on the job, on the other people who were always around them. But here, on this day devoted to celebrating the special relationship between a man and a woman, her defenses were down.

She had spent the entire wedding ceremony looking not at the bride and groom, but at Hagan, more handsome than ever in formal wear, though his expression throughout the ceremony remained as severe as his sharply tailored suit. This was not Hagan her coworker or even Hagan her friend, but Hagan the man who made her heart race and her knees weak. The Hagan who made her think about things besides skiing and her accident and her uncertain future. Hagan reminded her that beneath her ski patroller's uniform and her racer's bravado, she was very much a woman, with all a woman's needs and vulnerabilities.

That was the very worst of it—how vulnerable she felt with him now, as if he'd stripped away all her pretenses and seen her very core, the part of her that was afraid of failure, afraid of never realizing her dreams... afraid of being alone.

She was glad his height made it difficult to look into his eyes now. She fixed her gaze on his lapel, at the boutonniere of a white rosebud and baby's breath pinned there. But her mind scarcely registered the flower, all her senses focused instead on the weight of his hand at the small of her back, the heat of his body so close to hers, the starch-and-spice scent of him surrounding her.

"Why did you want to dance with me?" she asked.

"I felt like dancing."

She tilted up her head to look at him then. His expression was as calm as ever, betraying nothing. "But you don't usually dance," she said. "Not at the Eldo or at any of the parties where I've seen you."

His gaze met hers, the intensity of his look stealing her breath. "I wanted to dance with *you*," he said, and pulled her closer.

She surrendered to the moment, closing her eyes, a smile tugging on her lips. So much about this was wrong, impossible even. Hagan didn't date local women. He wanted nothing to do with any woman who might be in his life next week, never mind next year. He was a player who shunned commitment, a man whose true emotions were impossible to read.

And yet here they were, dancing around their feelings as much as they moved around the dance floor. He promised nothing except this one dance and she didn't dare to expect more. It would never be enough, but in this brief moment in time, it was everything.

The music stopped and they separated. Hagan looked as stunned as Maddie felt. He led her to the edge of the dance floor and cleared his throat. "Would you like another drink?" he asked.

"No. I think I'll find the ladies' room."

"If you will excuse me, I will have another drink."

She watched him walk away, tempted to make a quick exit. And then what? Go back to her apartment and anesthetize her feelings with a pint of rocky road ice cream?

Before she could act on her impulse to leave, Andrea came up to her. "What is going on with you and Hagan?" she demanded.

"Nothing," Maddie said automatically, even as she felt the blood rush to her face.

Andrea grinned. "You'd make a lousy poker player." She nudged Maddie in the side. "Come on, 'fess up. I saw you two dancing just now, and you looked very cozy."

"He asked me to dance, that's all."

"That's all?"

"He said he felt like dancing." She shrugged. "Maybe weddings make him sentimental or something."

Andrea clearly didn't believe any of this. "You're sure nothing's going on between you two?" she asked.

Nothing Maddie could put into words. Nothing she could begin to understand. "We're just friends," she said. Hadn't he made it clear that was all they would ever be, that he didn't need—or want—an intimate relationship with a woman that lasted longer than a few days? "It was only one dance." She stepped around Andrea. "Excuse me. I was just leaving."

Great. People had noticed them dancing. By nightfall the whole town would be speculating on what was happening between the two of them. No doubt there would be interesting theories, perhaps even bets made on how long before Hagan moved on to someone else. Others would shake their heads and feel sorry for the new girl who didn't know enough to stay away from a man for whom a long-term relationship was anything over three days.

In her car, she checked her reflection in the rearview mirror. Her face was flushed, her eyes bright. She looked like a woman who had just run a race—or one who had made love.

She bit back a moan of despair at the thought. What an idiot she was. She'd gone and lost herself to a man who was utterly unobtainable. There wasn't enough ice cream in the whole state of Colorado to soothe the ache this knowledge caused her.

Chapter Nine

Now that all the fuss of Heather and Ben's wedding was behind him, Hagan hoped his life would settle back into his normal routine. When Zephyr suggested some training runs in the resort's extreme terrain, he was only too glad to accompany him. Hurtling down the steeps and hucking off cliffs seemed the perfect antidote to the restlessness he had been feeling.

"The competition's only three weeks away, so I'm stepping up my training," Zephyr explained as he and Hagan rode to the top of Spellbound and Phoenix Bowls. "It really helps to have someone along to act as a spotter and critique my form."

They unloaded from the lift and started down the traverse trail toward the double black diamond and extreme-rated runs in the area. "So most of the snowboard competition is going to be in this area, right?" Zephyr said.

"Yes." Ski patrol had already been briefed. They would be providing coverage for all the events—not an easy task given the terrain they would be in. The steep cliffs, narrow chutes and tight trees made access to injured skiers difficult. Given the nature of the stunts skiers and boarders performed in the competition— jumping off twenty-foot cliffs was common—and the small margin for error, injuries could be severe. Helicopters and ambulances would be on call to transport severely injured participants to hospitals in Gunnison or even Denver, but immediate care and evacuation was the responsibility of ski patrol.

"Let's start with Highlife to Sun Steps to Dead Bob's Chute," Zephyr said. "What I think would work best is for you to go down first, kind of scout things out, then I'll follow and you can give me any pointers."

"Or radio for help if you crash," Hagan said.

Zephyr grinned. "That, too. Oh, and speaking of radios…" He reached back in his pack and pulled out two walkie-talkies. He handed one to Hagan. "Here you go, coach. When you get to the bottom, radio me any tips about the route I should take."

Hagan tucked the walkie-talkie into the pocket of his parka, then started down Highlife. The ungroomed run was steep, but fairly wide at the top. He turned into a landscape of thick trees and boulders on Sun Steps. He took his time getting down, navigating around obstacles, skidding and sliding at times. His objective was to get down safely, not to make a spectacular show of launching himself off tall boulders and cliffs.

Halfway down Sun Steps he stopped and radioed to Zephyr. "I did not see anything to worry about on Highlife. Lots of obstacles on Sun Steps. Your first jump is about a hundred yards in. You will have to tighten up and avoid the trees. Aim left."

"Roger that. Here I come."

He pocketed the radio once more and looked up the slope. On this weekday afternoon, he and Zephyr had the area to themselves. The sun was out, the snow was thick and soft, and the air was cold and crisp. It was paradise and he wouldn't trade a moment like this for all the desk jobs in the world.

He thought of his conversation with Maddie the day they had patrolled together. She was not the first to question why an intelligent man in his midthirties would choose a life many considered to be only one step above that of a ski bum.

Some understood the appeal of spending time out of doors, free to make his own decisions. But few guessed that it was everything this life lacked that drew him as much as all it offered.

Since coming to Crested Butte six years ago, he had fashioned a life that made few demands on his emotions or intellect. He had friends, but no one he was responsible for. He had freed himself from stress, worry and competition. And he had completely abandoned the identity he had once prized.

He was a different man now, and most of the time he forgot that other Hagan Ansdar had ever existed. Only lately had he thought more about the things he had turned his back on all those years ago: family, close ties…love. He had almost convinced himself he did not need any of those things—that they were not worth the price he had to pay to get them.

But was he right about that?

A few minutes later, Zephyr appeared above him, rocketing down the steep run with seeming reckless speed. But as he came closer, Hagan could see that each turn was executed with fierce control and precision. Zephyr paused for a moment at the jump, then launched himself into the air, landing with a soft whomp! in the thick snow ten feet farther down the run, clouds of powder billowing around him as he remained upright and blasted down the short, steep stretch to where Hagan stood.

"Most excellent!" Zephyr shouted as he skidded to a stop.

Hagan had to admit he was impressed. "You have been working hard," he said. "You looked like a pro up there."

Zephyr grinned. "Just 'cause I'm a rock star doesn't mean I can't be an athlete, too." Then his expression sobered. "I know some people around here think I'm a flake. I'd like to prove to them they've got me wrong. I'm serious about my music and I'm serious about this."

Some people or some *one,* as in a certain attractive coffee shop owner?

Hagan kept his mouth shut. He was not one to give advice about women. His own record was far from stellar. And lately he had had no record at all. He had lost all stomach for overpolished beauties and temporary flings. The result was an unaccustomed celibacy. He had spent the night alone in his cabin so much recently even Fafner was starting to give him odd looks.

They made their way down the rest of Sun Steps to a narrow, rocky chute that bore the macabre name of Dead Bob. This was not a run Hagan would have made for pleasure, but as he negotiated the tight turns and required jumps, his reward was a sense of satisfaction that he was up to the challenge.

Zephyr pushed himself to go faster and leap farther.

At one point he crashed into a tree and tumbled several yards, but he was back on his feet immediately, performing a perfect 360-degree turn with a backside grab on his next jump. He whooped and pumped his arms when he stuck the landing. "I'm psyched!" he declared when he met up with Hagan once more. "Bring on the competition, 'cause I am ready."

The tough terrain fed into a blue run off the East River Lift. From there they made their way to the North Face lift and more extreme terrain. They were poised at the top of Spellbound Glades when a shout caught their attention. Hagan looked back and was surprised to see Maddie skiing toward them.

"What are you doing here?" he asked. "Is something wrong?" Perhaps she had been sent to fetch him to respond to some emergency.

"Scott told me you were over here." She looked down the steep terrain spread out before them. "I thought if we're going to be patrolling here during the Free Skiing competition, I needed to get more familiar with the runs."

"Not every patroller will be here," he said. "You could ask Scott to assign you to other areas." He remembered her terror that day on Banana Peel and the reason behind it.

She gave him a sharp look. "I'm fine."

"Hey, Maddie. How's it going?" Zephyr gave her a high five.

"Great. You don't mind if I take a few runs with you two, do you?"

"Happy to have you," Zephyr said. He stretched his arms over his head. "Let's take it easy for a while. I need to loosen up a little after that last run."

He led the way into the glade, carving around trees, in no hurry. Hagan and Maddie followed. Hagan skied behind Maddie, keeping his eye on her. He sensed the tension radiating from her, but she hid it well.

Her shoulders were rigid, and she skied a little stiffly, skidding her turns, but she made it out of the glade with no real trouble. She stopped to catch her breath and Hagan joined her. "Stop staring at me," she said. "I'm fine."

He could have told her he could not stop looking at her even if he had wanted to. Whenever he was with her, his gaze was drawn to her, not in the way any man might look at a beautiful woman, but as if he *needed* to look at her, or feel emptiness inside him.

He said none of this, and after a moment, she skied on…and was stopped short at the top of a cliff a few yards away. "What is this run called again?" she asked.

"Body Bag," Zephyr said.

"Obviously named by someone with a sick sense of humor," she said.

"It's sick all right." Zephyr grinned. "Watch this." Not waiting for a reply, he launched himself off the cliff. Hagan heard the sharp intake of Maddie's breath, and instinctively put his hand to her back. She did not shake him off, and together they watched as Zephyr plummeted twenty feet onto a narrow steep. He landed crookedly, with a force that shook snow from nearby trees, the powder around him exploding in great billows, obscuring him from view. A few seconds later, he emerged with a shout, slid to the side and looked back up at them. "I nailed it!" he shouted.

"He did." Maddie looked back at Hagan. "That's insane. No way I'd even attempt that."

"Me, either." He clicked out of his skis. "Come on. We'll climb down."

They half climbed, half slid down the steep. Zephyr laughed at their approach. "You ought to try hucking it," he said. "There's no feeling like it."

"No thanks," Maddie said. "I was crazy enough to race down narrow, icy race courses, but I was never crazy enough to leap off cliffs like that."

"Come on," Hagan said, clicking back into his skis. "We can cut through the trees back over to Dead Bob."

"Dead Bob?" Maddie laughed, sounding shaky. "Do you think the map makers are trying to tell people something?"

"What would that be?" Zephyr asked.

"I don't know. Maybe only an idiot would ski a run called Dead Bob?"

Zephyr laughed and headed out in front of them. Maddie and Hagan followed at a slower pace. Hagan found himself tensing with her, holding his breath as she navigated a particularly narrow chute, stiffening his legs and mimicking her turns through a long, icy section. By the time they reached the top of Black Eagle, a groomed blue run, his legs were shaking and his fleece was soaked with sweat.

"I've got to book it," Zephyr said. "I've got band practice in half an hour." He slapped Hagan on the back. "Thanks for going with me this afternoon. You, too, Maddie. See ya."

With a wave, he took off, zipping down the run far too fast, but there were no crowds today, and Hagan and Maddie were off duty.

"Do you want to ski some more?" Maddie asked.

He shook his head. "No." What he wanted, suddenly, was food. "Are you hungry?" he asked.

She hesitated, then nodded. "I am."

"Then let us go eat."

Half an hour later, they were walking to the parking lot where Hagan had left his truck. "Where is your car?" he asked her.

"I took the shuttle," she said. A free shuttle made the loop of most of the condos around the resort.

"Put your skis in the rack with mine and I will drop you off at your place after we eat," he said.

Skis stowed, they climbed into his truck and he headed out of town.

Maddie was silent until they passed through Crested Butte. "Where are we going?" she asked.

"I wanted to get away," he said. Far from prying eyes who might speculate on why Hagan and Maddie were dining together. It was not a question he cared to consider too carefully himself.

During the drive they traded stories about happenings on the slopes and eventually he stopped the truck in front of a Mexican food place on the edge of Gunnison. This time of afternoon there was only one other vehicle in the parking lot and almost no chance of them running into anyone they knew.

Inside, the waitress led them to a booth, then brought chips and salsa, water and silverware. Hagan ordered a beer while Maddie opted for a diet soda. She looked around the nearly empty restaurant. "Do you come here often?" she asked.

He shrugged. "Sometimes." He picked at the label on the beer bottle, then added. "In a small town, where everyone knows everyone, it is natural to speculate on one another's business. Most of the time, that does not bother me. Sometimes it does."

She nodded. "Yeah. Me, too." She traced her finger through the condensation on the outside of her glass. "A couple of people said something to me about us dancing together at Ben and Heather's wedding."

He nodded. He had heard the comments, as well, and had ignored them. "Sometimes, when you have lived somewhere a few years, people think that they know you—that they can predict how you will behave. When you do not behave that way, they are…suspicious."

His choice of words earned a smile. "That's a good way to put it."

The waitress returned to take their order. They each chose enchiladas. When they were alone again, Maddie tilted her head and studied him. "So tell me about the Hagan other people don't know."

He opened his mouth to make some teasing remark to put her off, but instead felt an overwhelming urge to tell her the truth—a truth almost no one knew. "You already know I used to write computer software for a living," he said. "I was very good. One of the top pro-grammers in Oslo."

She blinked, obviously stunned. It surprised him, too, sometimes, to think back on that other life, so long ago. "Only a few years out of university, I was recruited by a high-tech firm in Austin, Texas, to work for them in the United States."

She nodded. "Is that how you ended up over here?"

"Yes." He took a long drink, contemplating how to fill in this next part: how much to reveal, what to leave out. "I was dating a woman at the time. We were living together, actually. We had been together six months by then. When I got the job offer, she suggested we marry, so that she could come with me to America."

Maddie's eyes widened. "You were married?"

He nodded. Inwardly he cringed, remembering how eager he had been to carry out the scheme. He had always been the more ardent of the two of them, though even in those early days he had suspected she might not be as faithful as he hoped.

But once he had accepted the new position in Austin, she became truly devoted to him. Her attentions had kept him in a constant fog of lust and daydreams about the future. She had talked of the children they would have, the life they would live.

He had never been happier.

"What happened?" Maddie asked. She looked away. "I'm sorry, it's really none of my business."

"I would not have brought it up if I did not want to tell you." He did want her to know, if only to share the burden of the secret he had kept for too long.

They were interrupted again by the arrival of their food. Neither of them said anything for long minutes as they ate. He hoped the food would give him the strength to go on. When his plate was half-empty, he ordered a second beer and looked at Maddie again. "Her name was Mista." A name he had not uttered aloud in years. Saying it now sent an uncomfortable quiver through him.

"That's a pretty name," she said.

"Hmm. She was a beautiful woman. Outside, at least." He sipped the beer, then continued. "We moved to Austin, to an expensive apartment near the river. I thought she would get a job, but she had trouble obtaining the proper visa. I learned later she had never applied and had lied to me about the paperwork." He frowned, remembering the arguments they had had, how guilty he had felt afterward for berating her about something that was not her fault. And how foolish he had felt later when he had learned the truth.

Maddie pushed her plate away. She had only eaten half her food. She sat back in the booth, her eyes fixed on him. Waiting.

He ate some more enchilada. He could hardly taste the spicy food, but eating gave him something to do with his hands, somewhere to look besides Maddie's face. "I had to travel some for my job. While I was away Mista would go out with friends. Girlfriends, I thought. Later I found out there were men. Several men." His hand tightened around his fork. One of the men had been a coworker of his, someone he considered a friend. For a while it had felt as if everyone he had ever trusted had betrayed him.

"Oh, Hagan." Maddie's voice was soft, full of sympathy, tinged with outrage.

He gave up on the food at last and pushed his plate aside also. "I did not know any of this at first. Meanwhile, my company sponsored me for a green card. Mista persuaded them to sponsor her, as well. After all, she was my wife, they wanted me to stay in the country…" He shrugged.

"And with a green card, she was able to stay in the country, whether the two of you were married or not," Maddie said.

He nodded. "Once she had the card, things changed," he said. "She was no longer happy with our marriage. With me." He made a fist, squeezing his fingers together until they ached, surprised that the old anger was still so strong. "One day I returned from a business trip and she was gone. I received divorce papers in the mail a week later."

"Oh, Hagan." The pain in her voice touched him.

He cleared his throat. "I did not take it well. I quit my job, gave up the apartment. I thought of going back to Norway, but it is a small country. Everyone in my field of work knew about us. To return and tell them she had only used me as her ticket to the United States..." He shook his head.

"You don't know that," Maddie said. "Maybe she did love you at first."

He shook his head. "No. The last time I saw her, on the day we signed the divorce papers, she told me she only wanted to come to the U.S., that she would never have married me otherwise." Her words had devastated him. He had felt burned up inside, a hollow shell. He went through the motions of living, but felt nothing.

"I eventually ended up in Colorado. I liked the mountains. I got work with the forest service, and then with the ski resort in winter." It had been healing, being out of doors. "Four years ago, I became a citizen."

He waited for Maddie to say something—to berate him for avoiding another relationship because of what had happened with Mista, or to comment on the irony of his reputation as a player, considering how his wife had played him. He knew all the pop psychology theories.

He also knew real emotions and motivations were seldom so easily summed up.

"I can't imagine how I'd feel if something like that happened to me," she said after a moment. "The last man I was serious about was an Italian ski racer—Dominic. I knew going in that he was a playboy. He used to say he loved women too much to limit himself to one." She shook her head. "But I was foolish enough to believe that with me, he would be different."

The sharp jealousy that lanced through him took Hagan by surprise. He had never heard of this Dominic person, knew nothing of his relationship with Maddie, yet the hurt in her eyes when she spoke of the man made Hagan want to strangle him.

The waitress brought their check, and he was grateful for the distraction of settling the bill, figuring the tip and gathering up their jackets to leave. Maddie excused herself to go to the ladies' room and Hagan took the opportunity to compose himself. He felt exhausted, drained both emotionally and physically. He had literally emptied himself to Maddie, and he could not say why, or what would happen now that he had done so.

Chapter Ten

Maddie washed her hands and studied her face in the too-yellow light of the ladies' room. She felt as shaky as if she'd downed three margaritas. Hagan *married?* She tried to imagine him as the man he'd described— young, idealistic. In love. She couldn't do it. He was *Hagan*—handsome, confident, distant and cynical.

And yet…

And yet, there *was* another man beneath that hard facade. *That* man was the one who'd held her that moonlit night when she'd been lost in the backcountry. That was the man who looked at her with concern in his eyes this afternoon on the extreme runs. It was a secret identity he kept well hidden.

Why had she told him about Dominic? As if an affair of a few months with an Italian playboy had any correlation to the end of a marriage. It was only that Dominic had hurt her, had made her wary around men, especially handsome men who had a reputation of using women as convenient accessories.

She turned from the mirror and dried her hands, too tired to analyze any of this further. She wanted to go back to her condo, take a hot shower and maybe watch a movie. Something light and uncomplicated that didn't require her to think too much.

They walked to his truck in silence and neither said anything on the drive back to Crested Butte. Fatigue dragged at her, but she was unable to surrender to sleep, every sense aware of the man beside him. The revelations of the afternoon had revealed an unsuspected vulnerability that made him all the more desirable to her. She had long ago ceased thinking of him as a shallow player—today she had seen that he had suffered the loss of his dreams not so different from her own loss. The future he'd dreamed of had been stolen from him.

She felt connected to Hagan more than ever now, and wondered what this boded for their future. She loved him, but he still felt out of reach, so she was stranded in this limbo of wanting him but being afraid to say so, hoping he would one day realize her feelings, or reveal his own desire for her.

He pulled into the parking lot behind her condo and they climbed out of the truck. He unlocked the rack and took down her skis while she collected her boot bag from the back. "Thank you," she said, feeling suddenly shy and awkward. All she really wanted was to throw her arms around him and hold him close, but she feared he'd flee at such a gesture. Instead, she took the skis from him and leaned them against the side of the vehicle, then turned to him once more.

She merely meant to kiss his cheek, an innocent gesture of both goodbye and thanks for his trust in confiding in her. But at the last moment he turned toward her and their lips met.

For an instant in time, she had never known such stillness. She was aware of her heart pounding in her chest, of the heat of his mouth against hers, of the overwhelming need to lean closer, to surrender to the desire that possessed her, overruling logic and sense and sanity. She was poised on the edge of a chasm, holding her breath, afraid to move for fear of either leaping or falling.

And then his arms went around her just as she reached for him. He crushed her to him and angled his mouth more firmly against hers, breathing in as if he might inhale her very essence.

It was the kiss of lovers, all open mouths and tangling tongues, their bodies pressed together from shoulders to knees. She stood on tiptoe, her hands clasped at the back of his neck, the soft ends of his hair brushing her fingertips, the slightly astringent smell of clean male sweat surrounding her.

He tasted of beer and peppers and a sweetness she couldn't define, and the gentle pressure of his mouth on hers sent heat shuddering through her. She arched against him, aware of the hard line of his erection against her stomach and the ever-growing tension of her own desire. Her mind raced. Was Andrea home? Did she dare invite him in?

A door slammed in the distance, and loud laughter drifted to them, the effect like ice water tossed over them. They jerked apart and stood, not touching, not looking at each other, only the sound of their ragged breathing breaking the silence between them.

Maddie was shaking, sure that the slightest word from him would cause her to laugh or weep or collapse in a heap at his feet. She risked looking at him through the veil of her lashes and saw he'd put his hand to his mouth. He was staring at the ground, with the look of a man in shock. "I—I had better go," he mumbled.

"Yes." Yes, he had better leave, before they both did something they'd regret. With trembling hands, she somehow managed to pick up the skis and the boot bag and wobble to the door of her condo.

She didn't dare look back, but she heard a car door slam, and the sound of the truck engine revving, then pulling away.

Safely inside the condo, she shoved the skis and bag into the front closet, then fled to her bedroom. She closed and locked the door, then slid to the floor, her back against the wall, eyes closed, every nerve still tingling from that amazing, incredible, confusing kiss.

HAGAN COULD NOT BELIEVE he had been so stupid. He had known all day that he was letting down his guard too much with Maddie, yet he had not found the will to stop himself. Something about the woman confounded all his usual defenses.

The only course of action left to him was avoiding her as much as possible. Given time, he was sure his overheated emotions would cool down and he would be in control again.

He changed his schedule at work, stopped going to the Eldo, and by the end of the next week was congratulating himself on successfully staying away from Maddie for ten days. On Friday he went out for pizza with Max to celebrate.

"What's your costume for the Masquerade Ball?"

Max asked as they waited for their pizza at a booth in the back of The Secret Stash on Elk Avenue.

Hagan stifled a groan. Normally Crested Butte's penchant for costumed spectacles was fun—a good excuse to cut loose and party. But lately it was all blurring together. "What is this one for, again?"

"Mardi Gras!" Max punched him in the shoulder. "Best party of the year. I'm thinking of going in drag."

Hagan looked at the burly six-footer. "I am sure you will be the belle of the ball."

Max laughed. "Casey's going to dress as a man. Role-reversal, get it?"

"People are going to wonder about 'his' taste in women."

"So what are you going as?" Max prodded.

"Maybe I will not go." He sipped his beer. For one thing, Maddie was sure to be there. And probably *not* dressed as a man. As if that would make any difference. The way they had almost scorched the paint on his truck with that kiss, she could be dressed as King Kong and he'd develop a sudden attraction to apes.

Their pizza was ready so Max went to retrieve it from the order window. He returned and slid it onto the table. "You don't show up, people are going to talk," he said as he helped himself to a big slice.

"Tell them I have the flu."

Max shook his head. "If you ask me, you've got woman trouble."

Hagan choked on a bite of pepperoni. He coughed and stared at Max. "Why do you say that?"

"I've known you, what? Six years now? Nothing

puts you in a bad mood like getting tangled up with the wrong woman. What is it this time? Jealous boyfriend?"

Hagan shook his head. "Nothing like that." He had not dated anyone in weeks.

"Jealous husband?" Max asked.

"No! I have some morals."

"Yeah, but there's no guarantee the lady is telling the truth. One of the hazards of dating strangers."

"It is nothing like that."

"Let's see." Max stared at the ceiling, as if the answer was written up there. "That leaves a woman who's getting too serious about you."

Was Maddie getting serious about him? She had made no move to seek him out this past week. And she had seemed as stunned as he had been by their kiss. The knowledge made him feel a little better—guilt had warred with self-preservation this week. He had told himself it was for the best if she thought he was a cad or a coward for staying away from her, but the idea that he might have truly hurt her had caused him more than a few sleepless nights.

"The way I see it," Max said, "costumes either play to type—in which case you'd come as Casanova—or they go against type. Hence my dressing in drag. I guess they could also represent wishful thinking—like the year Eric wore a Speedo and said he was a porn star."

Hagan had not been much of a Casanova lately. "What would my costume be if I played against type?" he asked, his curiosity aroused.

Max chewed and considered the question. "I'm not sure how you'd portray the settled, family man," he said after a moment. "*That* would be against type."

Hagan nodded. Once upon a time he had aspired to be just that. Too long ago, but Max's words had given him an idea—a costume that would be good for a laugh, if nothing else. "You have talked me into it," he told Max. "I will show up at the ball."

"So what's your costume?"

"You will have to wait until the party to find out." If Maddie saw it, she would know what it meant. It would be their own private joke. Maybe even a way for them to get back on a better footing as friends, not lovers.

MADDIE HAD CELEBRATED Mardi Gras on ski slopes in Italy, France and Switzerland. The holiday had been a brief respite from the rigors of competition and training. None of the festivities had been particularly memorable, unlike the Crested Butte party, which featured much revelry throughout the town, including tonight's Masquerade Ball. The costume she'd chosen had seemed fun back in her condo, but now she wasn't so sure.

As she stood with Andrea by the punch bowl in a room crowded with partiers, music and laughter echoing around them, she smoothed the glittery ruffles around the low-cut neckline of her outfit. "Maybe this is too much," she said, tugging at the very short skirt.

"You look great." Andrea, dressed as a dalmatian, complete with floppy ears and a shiny black nose, brushed glitter from one of Maddie's shoulders. "A lot of guys are looking this way, believe me."

She didn't want *a lot* of guys looking at her—only one. And so far she'd seen no sign of him.

In fact, she'd seen nothing of Hagan for days. She

knew he was still alive because she'd heard his voice on the radio at work, and seen his truck in the employee parking lot. But after two weeks without so much as a chance encounter on the ski runs, she had to believe he was avoiding her.

Obviously, the kiss had frightened him away. Neither of them had meant for that kiss—that incredible, scorching kiss—to happen.

"I wonder where Hagan is?" Andrea asked, as if on cue. "I haven't seen him around much lately, have you?"

Why was Andrea asking *her?* "No." She shook her head. "I haven't seen him, either."

"I wonder what's going on with him?" Andrea was studying Maddie now, as if watching for her reaction.

Maddie kept her expression placid. "What do you mean?"

"He used to have a different woman with him every weekend. Always tourists, and never the same one two weeks in a row."

The reminder annoyed Maddie. "Yeah. So?"

"So…the only one he's been seen with lately is *you.*"

"Hagan hasn't been with me," Maddie protested. She could feel a hot flush rising to her cheeks and hoped it was too dark for Andrea to notice.

"He danced with you at Heather and Ben's wedding."

"*One* dance."

Andrea leaned closer. "Eric said he was driving in to Gunnison one afternoon a couple of weeks ago and he saw Hagan's truck and it looked like *you* were with him."

Maddie looked away. "I can't believe people in this town are so interested in Hagan's personal life." Or hers.

"Were you with him?" Andrea persisted.

Maddie was saved from answering by the arrival of Bryan. He was dressed as a pirate, complete with a patch over one eye. "Want to dance, Andrea?" he asked.

She smiled. "Sure."

As Bryan led Andrea away, Maddie surveyed the scene in the crowded ballroom. She recognized almost everyone here, some in spite of—and some because of—their costumes. Trish was a mermaid with a seashell bra and shimmery green tail, while Zephyr wore oversized rubber waders and carried a large fishing pole.

Casey and Max were hilarious as each other—Max with a blond wig and an outrageous pink dress and heels and Casey with pasted-on sideburns, board shorts and one of Max's faded T-shirts.

Scott was a mad scientist in a stained lab coat while Heather and Ben wore matching Hawaiian shirts and water wings.

But Hagan was nowhere in sight. Somehow, the party didn't seem complete without his familiar presence. Maddie wished he was here while feeling glad he'd stayed away.

If he were here, she'd have someone to keep her company—why had she ever thought he was difficult to talk to? But now there was this physical awareness that made her heart race and breathing a little more difficult when she thought of him. She had to find a way to get past that. She didn't have so many friends she could afford to lose one because of a single moment of indiscretion. And neither of them needed the town's attention focused on them. As soon as they settled back into the roles of coworkers and casual friends, everyone's interest would turn elsewhere.

All her resolve abandoned her when she spied him standing in the doorway. Her heart fluttered wildly, even as she put one hand to her mouth to hold back a laugh.

He was dressed in white shoes and socks, a pair of horrible plaid pants that were at least six inches too short, a white short-sleeved shirt, polka-dot bow tie and a pair of black-framed glasses with duct tape at one corner. A plastic pocket protector with a row of ballpoint pens completed this ensemble.

Laughter followed him as he crossed the room, along with applause and shouts that he had won the costume contest, hands down.

It took a while for him to work his way over to Maddie. People kept stopping him to comment on his costume.

Her urge to laugh had subsided by the time he reached her. Awful clothes and all, Hagan was still a very good-looking man. If anything, the costume made him seem sexier, because of her knowledge of what the glasses and geek-wear poorly concealed.

"Hello, Maddie," he said when he reached her side.

"Nice costume," she said. She smiled, but avoided meeting his eyes.

"I thought you might appreciate it."

"I'm still having a hard time believing you ever were a real geek," she said.

"I promise you, I did not dress like this."

She told herself she was only imagining his gaze on her, then his fingers brushed the fluttery sleeve of her costume. "What are you supposed to be?" he asked.

She smoothed the short skirt. "An ice dancer."

"Why an ice dancer?"

That was the question of the night. Every costume had a story behind it, and the stories were part of the evening's entertainment. "The athletes on the ski team used to make fun of ice dancers," she said. She made a face. "Snotty of us, I know."

"There is not much costume there," he observed. He bent closer, his voice low in her ear. "But I like what I see."

Her mouth went dry, and she tried to swallow but failed. Unable to stop herself, she raised her eyes to meet his. It was like looking into a dark mirror at her own feelings. In Hagan she saw the same desperate intensity, the longing battling logic, desire winning over fear. Her heart pounded and every nerve tingled with the memory of their one kiss.

Determination and logic were obviously no match for whatever magic Hagan worked over her. She couldn't stay away from the man.

It was that same impulsiveness that always got her into trouble. Allowing her emotions to get the better of reason had ended her racing career and now that same recklessness had her mooning after a man who avoided emotional entanglement the way some people stayed away from heights or confined spaces.

She'd fallen for Hagan—hard and fast. And she knew it was going to hurt like hell when she finally hit bottom.

"Hagan, I think you've won the costume contest, hands down." Max walked up and slapped his friend on the back. "This is brilliant."

Casey was laughing so hard she had trouble talking. "Who would have ever thought of you as a geek?" she gasped between giggles.

Maddie realized she must be the only one there who knew about Hagan's past as a computer programmer. Apparently, he hadn't even told Max, his best friend.

So why had he trusted *her* with this knowledge?

She needed a time-out from thinking about such things. "Casey, do you mind if I dance with Max?" she asked.

"I don't mind." Casey looked at her fiancé. "I'm starting to feel weird dancing with another woman," she teased.

Max led Maddie onto the dance floor. The music was loud and fast, so they didn't have to talk. Max wasn't a very good dancer, but he was enthusiastic, and he looked so ridiculous in the wig and high heels she couldn't help but snicker.

"What's so funny?" he asked, feigning hurt.

"You!"

He acknowledged this comment with an exaggerated hip shimmy, almost knocking over the woman behind him. He apologized and managed to avoid further accidents until the song ended.

"Thanks for the dance," Maddie said as they made their way back to the punch bowl.

"You could have asked Hagan to dance with you," he said.

She dismissed the idea with a wave of her hand. "Oh, you know he rarely dances." Though he'd made an exception once. For her. Again a voice in her head asked *Why?*

Hagan and Casey were no longer by the dessert buffet. "They probably went to look for a table," Max said. "I'm thirsty. Want some punch?"

"Sure." She was pretty confident the drink was spiked but what the heck? It was Mardi Gras, after all.

He handed her a cup of punch. "Hagan is a riot in that getup," he said. "Where did he get those awful pants?"

She shook her head. "They are pretty terrible." She glanced at Max. "Can I ask you a question? About Hagan?"

His expression grew serious. "You can ask, but I may not answer."

"Do you know why he never dates local women?" Even though she knew the answer, this was the perfect opportunity to get insight into Hagan from his best friend. Plus, the male perspective was always illuminating.

He shrugged. "He doesn't want to get involved. Get tied down." He glanced at her. "Some men are like that. I thought I was. Why? Are you falling for him?"

She almost choked on her punch and had to look away. "Of course not." She felt shaky inside but when she raised the cup to her lips, her hand was steady. "I just think it's odd." And odd, too, that Max didn't know about Hagan's marriage. Or maybe he did know and was being a good friend and keeping mum.

Andrea and Casey waved to them from a table near the stage. "There they are," Max said, and started forward.

"I'll be right over. I just need to do something," Maddie said. She set aside her half-empty cup and made her way through the crowd to the door.

But she had no real intention of joining them at the table. She had to get out of here altogether, before she did or said something she regretted.

Maybe she was being a coward, but she couldn't face an evening of being near Hagan and trying to ignore the feelings that surged through her. She had to stay away from him until she could control herself better.

The man had been honest with her, letting her know all the reasons a relationship between them would never work. And now she had to listen to him and had to stop herself from falling further. She wasn't going to make the mistake she'd made in the past. This time, she wasn't going to act without thinking. She wouldn't let emotion get the better of wisdom and ruin her life a second time.

HAGAN WAS EMERGING from the men's room when he spotted Maddie in the hall. Her costume—what there was of it—was downright distracting. He told himself he would be safe from his feelings at a crowded party, yet here they were in this deserted hallway. It would be all too easy to pull her into a dark corner and satisfy his almost overwhelming desire to repeat the kiss they had shared.

Maybe she was feeling the same thing, because she took a step back when he hailed her. "Hagan!" she said brightly. "That is an amazing costume."

He glanced down at the absurd high-water pants and white shirt. "Do you believe now I was a geek?"

Her smile was genuine now, softer, as if she was re-membering the confidences they had shared. "You may have been the real thing, but even in that getup, you don't look like any geek I ever met."

"Just as well I left that line of work, since my image could not match my profession."

She pretended to consider the question. "Yes, you do look more like a recruiting poster for ski patrol. Although not tonight."

It was not only his costume that made him feel more in touch with his old life tonight. This afternoon he had sent an e-mail to his old friend, David. With his nights free since he had curtailed his social life, Hagan had been spending more time designing new programs and had mentioned them in his message.

To his surprise, David had asked to see Hagan's work. I always need good freelancers, he had written. It's nice to know you're keeping your hand in. You were always one of the best.

The praise had warmed him—a surprise in itself. He had thought himself long past such things.

He started to tell Maddie all this, then thought better of it. She already knew too many of his secrets. Better to keep something for himself.

She glanced around, as if to verify they were alone, then looked him in the eye, her expression serious. "Tell me why you've been avoiding me."

He opened his mouth to deny it, then realized the stupidity of such a lie. "I thought we needed some space to cool things off. What happened the other day outside your condo—"

"The kiss? You can say it, you know."

He nodded. "All right. When we kissed. I never meant for that to happen."

"I know. I didn't, either." She smiled. "Though it was a pretty amazing kiss."

His heart beat faster at the memory. "Yes. It was. But better that we do not repeat the experience."

She nodded, but said nothing.

He watched her eyes, trying to gauge if she was angry or hurt. He did not want her to think he was rejecting her. But she remained calm. Almost too calm. He had experience dealing with hysterical women—the occasional female who did not take kindly to his saying goodbye. Then there were the ones who were in a hurry to get away from *him*. Maddie's absolute serenity was new territory.

"It has nothing to do with you," he said, knowing this was the beginning of a bad cliché. "But we work together. We both live in this small town. I want to keep you as a friend, not end up as enemies."

She nodded, her expression never changing. "You're right." She reached out and touched his wrist—a light touch, but he swore his skin burned where her fingers brushed against him. "I like you, Hagan. Your friendship means a lot to me and I don't want to lose it, either. So don't worry. You don't have to avoid me."

"Good." He offered a small smile. "I have missed you."

"I've missed you, too." She squeezed his wrist, then released him. "That kiss will be our little secret."

Right. One more secret to add to his store. One more thing that he and Maddie shared.

Chapter Eleven

The Free Skiing Championship was four days of barely organized chaos at Crested Butte Mountain Resort. The reporters arrived first, on Wednesday: a film crew from ESPN and print media from *Sports Illustrated* and the various publications devoted to skiing and snowboarding.

Since most of the athletes hadn't yet arrived at the resort, the reporters occupied themselves filming scenery and interviewing anyone they could find who was associated with the event, including ski patrollers. Which was how Maddie found herself in the cafeteria at the base area with the ESPN newsman.

He introduced himself as Randy Milligan, then said, "I recognize you. You're Maddie Alexander, from the U.S. women's ski team."

There was no sense denying it; she wore a name tag that clearly identified her as Maddie A. "Yes," she said warily, praying her radio would go off and she could make a quick escape.

"This is terrific," Randy said, taking out a notebook. "I'd love to interview you, find out what you've been up to lately."

"Oh, I don't think so." She shook her head and looked past him, searching for a familiar face she could use as an excuse to leave.

Randy put his hand on her arm, his voice low, confiding. "You could really help me out of a jam here," he said. "I promised my boss I'd get some great background features for the games and so far I've come up with nada. My butt is in a sling here and you could really save me." His smile was ingratiating. "What could be better? A puff piece on what one of America's Skiing Sweethearts is up to now."

She grimaced at the hated appellation. She was nobody's sweetheart anymore, and had no desire to be reminded of her glory days.

Just then, the door to the cafeteria opened and a familiar tall figure entered. Hagan and Maddie had continued to keep a careful distance from each other since last week's costume ball, but right now he was a welcome sight. "I have to go," she told Randy, gently removing his hand from her arm. She gave him an apologetic smile. "I'm sorry, I really don't think I'd be a very interesting subject for an interview."

Before Randy could argue further, she hurried to Hagan's side. "Do you know anything about our assignments for the Free Skiing competition?" she asked, as if they'd last spoken only a few minutes—instead of a few days—before. "Scott hadn't posted them when I checked this morning."

Hagan's gaze was decidedly chilly. "No," he said. "Do you want to know so you can tell your friend there?"

"My friend?" She was puzzled, then realized he was

referring to Randy. She laughed. "He's not my friend. He's a reporter. I—"

"It is none of my business, anyway," he said, and turned away.

She stared at his back, a hot flush stinging her cheeks. What was Hagan talking about? Did he think she'd been cozying up to a reporter? And was it the reporter or the cozying that he objected to?

She looked back at Randy, who smiled and started toward her again. Hagan was already headed out the door. Maddie ground her teeth together, minor annoyance quickly churning into anger. The man was infuriating. He'd made it clear he wasn't interested in anything resembling a romantic relationship with her, and yet he objected to her so much as *talking* to another man?

Randy reached her side again, all smiles. "All I'm asking is maybe ten minutes in front of the camera," he said. "You can talk about your job here at the resort, about the valuable contribution ski patrol makes to the Free Skiing Championship, things like that. It'll all be very relaxed. You'll forget the camera is even there."

She wasn't worried about being nervous on camera. In her "sweetheart" days she'd given hundreds of interviews to journalists from all over the world. Somewhere in the family basement her parents had literally hours of footage of her on various television shows, from Jay Leno to an Austrian skiing special. She'd been a favorite of reporters because she was so good on camera.

The memory cheered her. She could use some ego stroking right now—and the chance to show Hagan that she wasn't wasting her time sitting around and mooning over him. She smiled at Randy. "I'd love to do the interview," she said. "Just tell me where and when."

HAGAN WAS CROSSING the parking lot on his way to his truck that evening when Max and Zephyr hailed him. "Come have a beer with us," Max said. It was exactly the distraction Hagan had been looking for.

Ten minutes later they were parked in the back of the Avalanche bar with full mugs arrayed before them. "Been taking some more practice runs?" Hagan asked Zephyr.

"Yeah. Max has been spotting for me. Two more days to showtime."

"Do you think you are ready?" Hagan asked.

Zephyr nodded. "I'm good."

"Let's order some grub," Max said. "I'm starved."

"Do you not have a fiancé to eat with?" Hagan asked.

"She and Heather are interviewing caterers or something like that." He waved over the waitress and asked for menus.

"Are you nervous about the wedding?" Zephyr asked.

"No, I'm just ready to be married." Max leaned back and stretched out his arms and yawned. "I never thought I'd say this, but I'm really ready to settle down," he said. "To have a little more permanence in my life."

Permanence. The word tugged at Hagan. He had told himself it was something he never wanted again, but maybe it was natural as a man got older to want a certain stability.

Not that he was old. At thirty-four, he was in his prime. But he had felt anything but settled lately.

The waitress returned with the menus and they ordered burgers and refills on the beer. "Hey, did you hear Maddie is going to be on TV?" Zephyr asked when they were alone again.

"No kidding?" Max said. "When?"

"Tomorrow evening, on ESPN. Some reporter is interviewing her tomorrow morning."

Hagan remembered the reporter—a man with immovable hair and too-white teeth who had been chatting up Maddie earlier that day in the cafeteria. Hagan knew he had been a real ass when he had accused her of being too friendly with the guy. He had immediately regretted the remark, but had seen no way to apologize without making things worse.

"We ought to get together and have a viewing party," Zephyr said.

"That's a great idea," Max said.

"Yeah." Zephyr grinned. "We have a real celebrity in our midst."

"The town is full of celebrities, here for the Free Skiing Championship," Max pointed out.

"Yeah, but Maddie is one of us now," Zephyr said. "A local."

Zephyr would no doubt include Hagan as a local, too, and it was true he felt as at home here as he ever had. But was a solitary cabin in the woods and a stray cat all he wanted for his life?

When he had first come to Crested Butte he had seen it as a temporary stopover on his way to the rest of his life. But the longer he stayed, the harder it was to move on, to get on with whatever the rest of his life would be.

"So what do you think of having a viewing party for Maddie's TV appearance?" Zephyr asked him.

Hagan shrugged. "Fine by me." At least he could get away with staring at her on television, something he was constantly steeling himself against in real life.

"Good, then can you get us the use of the conference room with the big-screen TV?"

"Why me?"

"Because you're the big ski patrol dude, and the only one of us who works for the resort," Zephyr said. "And because the person in charge of bookings is Tami Zamora and you can charm her into letting us use the room for cheap—or even free."

"I do not even know this Tami person."

"Doesn't matter." Zephyr shrugged. "She's female, sure to fall under your spell."

That was how they saw him, was it not? A man who could have any woman he wanted.

Except the one he wanted most.

MADDIE THOUGHT the interview went well. Randy had asked her about her work with ski patrol, her life in Crested Butte, and had said almost nothing about her former career or the accident that had ended it.

And now she had the viewing party to look forward to. She was pleased her friends had organized this celebration for her, touched they'd gone to so much trouble at a time when everyone was busy with the championship, which had begun in earnest this morning. Zephyr's snowboarding event would take place tomorrow and many of the same people who filled the conference room this evening would no doubt be there.

When she walked into the room she was greeted with shouts of welcome. She marveled at how, after only a couple of months, she no longer felt like an outsider here. Crested Butte was home now, and these people gathered around her were like family.

"We've got a reserved seat for you right up front," Zephyr said, escorting her to a plush chair in front of the big-screen TV that had been commandeered for the occasion. Other chairs, sofas and ottomans had been arranged around the television, and someone had even provided popcorn and drinks.

Casey and Max were there, along with Bryan, Trish, Patti, Heather and Ben. The ski patrollers arrived as a group: Andrea, Scott, Eric, Marcie and others. Maddie looked for Hagan and spotted him standing at the back of the room; she quickly turned away.

"Shh, everybody. It's time." Zephyr dimmed the lights and turned up the sound on the television as Randy Milligan's smiling face appeared. Maddie settled back in her chair, a flutter of nervousness rising in her chest.

"Tonight we continue with our series of 'Where are they now?' pieces with a look at one of the most promising American female skiers in the past decade," Randy began. "Maddie Alexander was part of the America's Sweethearts team expected to bring home the gold at the 2006 Olympic Winter Games in Torino, Italy. She'd already broken records on the World Cup circuit and had a reputation as one of the most daring— some said reckless—skiers on the U.S. team. Then in one horrifying moment on an icy mountain in St. Moritz, Switzerland, Maddie Alexander lost it all."

The scene on the television switched to footage of a

fog-shrouded mountain. As the camera zoomed in to show crowds gathered along a race course, Maddie felt as if a tremendous weight were pushing her down into her chair. She watched in growing horror as a close-up showed her own small figure, in her trademark helmet painted with clouds and the red, white and blue racing uniform of the U.S. team. She rocked back and forth in the starting gate, radiating energy and nerve.

Sitting here in her chair, her hands curled around the arms of her chair, but it was graphite racing poles she felt, and her toes pressed against the ends of her shoes as if they were ski boots. All the reflexes ingrained in her over the years were still there, every sensation rushing back as she watched the figure on the screen rocket out of the gate down the icy course.

The only sound was the chatter of her skis on the hard surface as she swept through the first sharp turns, her body almost parallel to the ground. Her muscles tensed with the memory of the effort it took to power through those turns.

She rounded a tight curve, flailed slightly, then righted herself, faster than ever. The sun that had spot-lighted the top of the course had been swallowed up in fog and blowing snow. Her mind played back the picture she'd memorized from the morning's inspection run: here was the straightaway, where she tightened her tuck and let her skis run, flying like a bullet, the world a white blur as she raced down the icy track.

Here was a hard curve where she laid almost over onto her side, only the edges of her skis remaining in contact with the ground, her muscles screaming in protest as she held the torturous posture.

Then she was upright again, traveling faster than ever. This next section was the trickiest, the one her coach had warned her to be careful with. She hadn't been afraid; she had long ago learned to lock the fear away so that it played no part in any race.

Instead of pulling back, she tucked tighter, soaring ever faster into the jump that marked the beginning of the second half of the course. She had no memory of what happened next, but she had watched the film many times—the same film that was playing now to the horrified gasps of her friends around her.

The figure on the screen soared over the bump, but came down at the wrong angle, a doll hurled to the ground by a temperamental child. She bounced sickeningly, a tangle of arms, legs, skis and poles, then bounced again and skittered, coming to a stop against a stretch of orange safety fencing. Maddie stared, unblinking, dry-mouthed, as the screen went black.

Randy's face appeared, his expression grave. "Maddie Alexander survived that horrific crash, and went on to ski again. But she lost something else that day in St. Moritz—she lost her nerve. The woman who had been one of America's greatest hopes for Olympic glory was now a failure."

The picture on the screen switched to Maddie yesterday afternoon, seated in a hotel suite, dressed in her red ski patroller's jacket, looking fresh and healthy. Not like a failure. But Randy's words echoed in her brain like shouts of accusation: *failure, failure, failure.*

She gripped the arms of the chair, white-knuckled, trying to quell the tremors that radiated through her. Her stomach churned and her lungs felt scorched. Someone murmured words of sympathy. Someone else put a gentle hand on her arm. Sound and vision blurred and she could sit still no longer. With a strangled cry, she lunged from the chair and ran from the room, ignoring the calls of those who came after her.

She ran, feet pounding on the carpeted floor—down a flight of stairs, across an empty locker room. She had no destination in mind, she only wanted to escape, to get away from the awful memories and the pity. She'd finally started to feel happy about her new life here, and now this reminder of all she'd left behind had destroyed every one of those good feelings. She'd failed at the only thing that had ever really mattered to her. How could she have possibly thought she'd be happy again?

HAGAN PUT OUT A HAND to stop Maddie, but she flew past him, unseeing. Around him, people were all talking at once. "I should go after her," Andrea said.

"No, leave her alone," Max said. "She's too upset to talk to anyone."

"I'd like to find that reporter dude and punch him," Zephyr said. "Talk about a dirty way to treat somebody."

Hagan said nothing, but left the room and started walking. Max was right—Maddie probably wanted to be alone right now. But he had to see for himself that she was all right.

He lost track of time as he wandered the empty halls of the building, then out into the icy darkness. A bitter wind sent snow swirling around his feet, icy shards hitting his cheeks. Head down, shoulders hunched, he kept walking, watching for Maddie.

He found her at a bus stop, a solitary figure standing apart from a laughing crowd of vacationers. He approached her without speaking. She looked at him, giving him a brief glimpse of her stricken face, then she turned away.

"Maddie—" he began.

She shook her head, warning him off. The lively, laughing woman he had known, the woman who had led the torch parade, the one who had raced ahead of him down snowy slopes, had been replaced by this shrunken, wounded figure.

Rage at those who had done this to her almost overwhelmed him. He wanted to strike out at something, to hurt anyone who had hurt her.

Instead, he wrapped his arms around her and held her tightly, trying to communicate what he had no words for.

She did not resist, but pressed her face against his chest and leaned her weight against him in mute surrender. He rested his chin on top of her head and closed his eyes, shutting out the world, focusing on her heart beating steadily against his, on the warmth shared between them and the sensation that time had stopped.

The spell was shattered by the squealing brakes of the bus as it approached. Maddie pulled away from him. "I have to go."

He put a hand on her arm, stopping her. "Come back to my cabin with me," he said.

Her eyes met his, wary. "Are you sure?"

He nodded. "Yes. Come with me. Please."

Chapter Twelve

The drive to Hagan's cabin was a silent one. He didn't attempt to fill the space with meaningless small talk and he didn't mention her television disgrace at all, for which Maddie was grateful. Even sympathy or outrage on her behalf would have been too much to bear just now.

She welcomed the companionable peace between them. Back there at the bus stop, standing in the shelter of Hagan's strong arms, her agitation and despair had eased somewhat, replaced by numb acceptance. That one grand mistake on the mountain in St. Moritz, captured on film to be replayed over and over whenever anyone thought of her, was the moment by which people like Randy Milligan would define her life.

The question now was whether she would define herself by that moment also.

She studied Hagan's reflection in the dark windshield—the strong line of his jaw, the jut of his nose, his well-shaped mouth. Within ten minutes of meeting him she had thought she knew him: too handsome for his own good, supremely confident, intimidatingly masculine, athletically gifted and emotionally stunted. She had seen his type before—men for whom women were delightful playthings to be used and discarded, but never taken seriously. Men for whom everything in life came easy, so that they had no understanding of true hardship.

How wrong she had been. No one in Crested Butte had shown more compassion and understanding for her than Hagan. And perhaps no one more than she knew his more vulnerable side.

He turned off the highway onto a rutted forest road that climbed up into the trees. As the truck groaned and rumbled over twin channels between thick walls of snow, Maddie stared into the absolute blackness ahead of them. She had never seen such impenetrable darkness.

After half an hour he turned down an even narrower track and within a few minutes stopped. The lights of the truck illuminated a small log cabin squatting in a clearing like a gingerbread cottage, the roof thickly iced with snow. "Come on," Hagan said. "I will start a fire, then make us a drink."

She followed him up a narrow path and into the cabin. She had steeled herself for the messy clutter of most of the other bachelor quarters she'd visited, but once again Hagan surprised her. His home was clean and uncluttered, almost spartan in its furnishings, yet every piece seemed chosen both for comfort and usefulness. A leather sofa and side table were arranged before the wood stove and behind them sat a wooden table and two ladder-back chairs. A desk was tucked into one corner, a computer monitor on it glowing softly.

Stairs led to a loft which probably served as his bedroom.

"Have a seat," he said. He opened the door of the wood-stove and began filling it with wood from a box nearby.

Maddie sank onto the sofa. After a moment, she felt something soft against her leg and looked down into an inquisitive feline face. "I didn't know you had a cat," she said. Yet another surprise.

"That's Fafner," he said, with no further explanation.

Fafner hopped onto the sofa and began sniffing at her. Apparently satisfied that he'd checked her out thoroughly, he walked to the other end of the sofa, curled into a ball, and watched as Hagan built the fire.

When the blaze was going well, Hagan turned to her again. "Would you like a hot drink?"

"Yes," she said. "That would be great."

While he busied himself in the small kitchen at the back of the cabin, Maddie continued to look around, searching for clues about Hagan's personal life. The room revealed little beyond a penchant for neatness and comfort. There were no photographs, and only a few decorations: a pair of old skis over the door and a ceramic stein on a shelf by the stove.

To her relief, there were no signs of other women, at least in these downstairs rooms—no photographs, no feminine articles of clothing left lying about, no hint of perfume in the air. Of course, she already knew Hagan had no steady girlfriend, but until recently, he almost always had some woman he was dating. Apparently none of them had succeeded in making a mark on this masculine retreat.

He returned and handed her a steaming mug. She

cradled it in her hands, the warmth seeping into her chilled fingers. He set a twin mug on the table beside the sofa and stripped off his jacket. "Do you want me to take your coat?" he asked. "The house is warmer now."

"Yes, thank you."

She took off the coat and he hung it beside his on a peg near the door, then sat beside her on the sofa. "How did you find this place?" she asked.

"The land belongs to the forest service, leased to the cabin owner for forty years," he said. "The old owner died and his heirs wanted to get rid of it. In the summer I work as a seasonal ranger and I heard about it my first summer here. It was a good price, so I bought it and spent the rest of the summer fixing it up for winter."

"It's very…private," she said. *Isolated* had been her first choice of word, but she didn't want him to think she was criticizing his home.

"I like being out of the way," he said. "In fact, you are the first woman who has ever been here."

This revelation startled her so much she was momentarily speechless. To cover her discomfort, she sipped at the drink. It was hot chocolate, liberally laced with Baileys. The sweet, rich concoction warmed her through. She was flattered Hagan was willing to share his sanctuary with her, but she couldn't think what it meant.

"Thank you," she said after a moment. "For the chocolate, and for bringing me here. I really didn't want to be alone after…after what happened this evening."

He turned toward her, his calm manner and expression putting her even more at ease. "I take it you had no idea the reporter was going to do that," he said.

"Call me a failure?" She made a face. "No. He told me we were going to talk about my work with the ski patrol, life in Crested Butte, all of that. I realized he would probably make some mention of my accident, but never that he'd show the film and make so much of it." Two years had passed since the accident, more than that since the *Sports Illustrated* cover. She had thought people would have forgotten about her by now.

"When I saw the look on your face as you left the room…" Hagan's voice was hard, his body rigid with anger. "I think if he had been there at that moment I could have killed him."

The sudden change in his demeanor and the heat of his words startled her. "He wouldn't be worth that," she said softly.

"Maybe not, but I was angry enough to at least break his jaw." His eyes met hers once more. "I could still do it, if you wanted me to."

She put a hand on his arm. "No. But thank you." She'd never want someone to do violence on her behalf, but she appreciated the chivalry behind the offer.

They sipped from their mugs in silence for a while. Maddie stared through the glass door of the stove at the flames licking the logs. She understood why Hagan liked this place. She felt safe here, far removed from the problems and concerns of everyday life.

"You are not a failure, you know."

The words startled her from her reverie. The steel in his voice sent a tremor through her. She drank more chocolate, wanting to blame the fluttering in her stomach on the liquor, and kept her eyes on the fire. "Thank you, but I felt like a failure after the accident," she said. "I had so much talent, years of training, so much promise, and I threw it all away in a single moment of impulsiveness." She looked away. "And then I didn't have the courage to compete again."

She could feel his gaze on her. Steady. Unjudging. "The recovery must have been brutal," he said after a moment.

She nodded. "It was. My hip was shattered, so they replaced it with an artificial joint. There's a titanium plate holding my leg bones together, and a bunch of screws in other places." She made a face. "I won't be modeling swimsuits anytime soon. I've got some scary looking scars."

"It sounds as if you were lucky to keep your leg."

She nodded. "I spent six weeks in the hospital, then another six months in a rehab facility. At first the doctors told me I'd be lucky to walk again, much less ski. I was determined to prove them wrong."

"That took a lot of courage," he said.

She shook her head. "It wasn't courage. I was just stubborn. I wanted to get back out there. To ski that course at St. Moritz again. To do it right this time." She set down her empty cup and turned to him. "I worked four months learning to ski again, getting back up to speed on the snow. I told my coach I was ready, so he met me at Park City, on the Olympic course there. The idea was to time me, to see if I was back in racing shape."

She squeezed her hands into fists, her stomach clenching also at the memory. "I was fine. Excited.

Looking forward to this moment I'd been working toward for the past year. I was thrilled to be back in the gate again. And then I stood there, looking down on the course and…" She opened her hands wide and shook her head. "I lost it. I just…fell apart. I was suddenly terrified. I tried to make myself ski down the run, but I was slow, my form was horrible."

"I am sure you are not the first," Hagan said.

"No. My coach said it happens sometimes. After a bad injury, a skier loses her nerve. But knowing I wasn't alone didn't make me feel any better. And time hasn't helped. You saw how I was up there that day on Peel. Whatever courage I had is gone."

His hand clamped around her wrist, and his voice was stern. "Do not tell me you do not have courage," he said. "What you have done—coming here and starting life over, making friends and getting on with living—takes a special kind of courage. One not everyone has."

She stared at him, not sure how to take his words. "You really think I'm brave?"

He released her wrist and rested the back of his hand against her cheek. She fought the urge to lean into that gentlest of caresses. "I do," he murmured, and bent to kiss her.

This was a kiss without the fever or urgency of their embrace in the parking lot three weeks ago, yet the very tenderness of it sent a tremor of desire burning through her. His lips brushed hers, then too soon were gone.

She opened her eyes and drew a shaky breath. "Why did you bring me here tonight?" she asked.

He looked at her for a long moment, his gaze steady, his eyes dark with some inner turmoil. "I wanted to protect you from people like that reporter," he said finally. "To hide you away where they could not reach you."

So he had brought her to the place where he hid himself away from whatever had the potential to hurt him. "But you said you never bring women here."

"I do not. But you are not one of those women."

She struggled to interpret what this might mean. She was not a tourist? She was not a woman he slept with? She was not a woman he would use and discard? "Hagan, I—" She closed her mouth, swallowed, and tried again. "I want to stay with you tonight."

He blinked. "I do not know if that is a good idea."

"Why not?"

He looked down. She could feel him pulling away from the connection they shared and she wanted to reach out and snatch him back. "I do not think I could have you here all night and keep my hands away from you," he said.

She bit back a smile of triumph, and desire stirred low in her abdomen. "I don't want you to keep your hands away from me." She leaned over and touched his arm. "I want to spend the night in your bed. With you."

His eyes met hers once more and she felt stripped naked by the desire that burned there. "I cannot promise anything more than tonight," he said.

"I know that." She didn't care about anything but tonight. The future was some far-off, amorphous dream while she and this man she wanted more than anything were here now. Alone, and with no good reason she could see not to take comfort in each other.

The hesitation she saw in his expression as he processed her answer was enough for her. She leaned forward and kissed him again, openmouthed, her lips hard against his, her arms slipping around him, pressing her body against him.

That was all he needed to let go of his last reserve. With a muffled groan he crushed her to him, his hands stroking, his lips seeking, until she was breathless and trembling.

Just as suddenly, he broke off the kiss and stood and hauled her to her feet. "The bedroom is upstairs," he said, his voice rough-edged.

She followed him up the steps to the loft, where a large bed with a headboard carved with wheat sheaves nearly brushed the ceiling. "The bed is from Norway," he said when he saw her staring at it. "It was a wedding present from my parents."

And perhaps no other woman had lain here with him since his wife. The thought sent a fresh wave of nervousness through her, but she pushed it aside and turned her attention to the man in front of her. He pulled off his sweater, then reached to help her off with hers. Standing at the foot of the bed, they took turns helping each other undress. Her shyness soon vanished in a rush of desire as she looked at him.

Truly, she had never seen a more perfect male body, and yet it was the tenderness in his touch, and the gentleness in his eyes when he looked at her that made her want him so much.

He held out his arms and she came to him once more, this time without the barrier of clothing between them. She ran her hands across the corded muscle of his back and arms, while he caressed the softness of her breasts and bottom. He trailed kisses along her neck and shoulders, breathing words of endearment almost too soft for her to hear.

When she was sure she could stand his attentions no more, that her knees would give way and she would sink to the floor, he helped her to climb into the high bed and beneath the quilts piled there. The sheets were cold against her fevered skin, but she scarcely noticed as he pulled her close once more.

This time he kept his eyes open, and trailed his hands slowly down her arm, over the curve of her hip to her thigh. There he lingered, tracing the scars from her various surgeries with the lightest of touches, as if he feared hurting her.

She had never felt so…revered before, and the unexpected tenderness surprised tears from her. Blinking rapidly, she slid down farther beneath the covers, and boldly reached for him. "I've been waiting weeks for this," she said. "I don't want to wait much longer."

He grinned. "You will have to wait a little longer." Then he slid from the bed and hurried into the adjacent bathroom. He was back in a moment, and when he reached the bed he opened his clenched fist to reveal a gold foil packet.

She laughed. "Nice to know you're prepared."

While he sheathed himself with the condom, she lay back, anticipating the fulfillment of a fantasy that she could admit now had been in the back of her mind almost from the day they met. Hagan was the type of man to conjure such fantasies in a woman, but something more than his looks and masculinity had drawn her to him. Maybe it was because beneath his bravado, she recognized a kindred spirit. Someone who had had great dreams and had given them up. He had dreamed of a happy marriage and a prosperous career. She had aimed for Olympic glory. Neither had gotten what they wanted.

But they could have each other. She smiled up at him as he leaned over her. She'd expected him to be as anxious as she was to get on with things, but he paused a moment, looking down at her as if memorizing her features.

Then he lay back beside her once more and reached for her. "We do not have to hurry," he said, stroking the side of her breast, sending shivers of desire through her. "We have all night."

From her breasts, he moved to her stomach, then to her thighs, fingers brushing and circling, awakening nerve endings she hadn't even known existed. Slowly, oh, so slowly, he circled upward. Her breath quickened with each stroke.

When he touched the thatch of curls between her thighs, she made a sound like a whimper, and he quieted her with a kiss, even as his fingers began to work in earnest, stroking, plucking, slipping inside her.

His mouth moved to her breast and she closed her eyes and arched against his hand, abandoning herself to the sensation of heat and light building within her. She brought one hand up to thread her fingers through his hair, while the other hand clutched at the sheets, the tension building within her.

Her climax shuddered through her in a deep, satisfying wave. Hagan moved quickly over her, and entered her before the last tremors faded away. The sensation of him filling her produced a new wave of arousal, and as he began to move with deep, even strokes she opened her eyes to look up at him, entranced by the sight of his handsome features transformed by desire.

She smoothed her hands down his back, tracing the indentation of each vertebrae, then stroked across his buttocks, down the rock-hard line of his thigh. He moved faster now, and she arched to meet him on each stroke, thrilling to the dizzying rush of her own fast-approaching release.

He came with a hoarse cry and she followed soon after. They rocked together a little while longer, holding each other tightly, eyes shut, unwilling to move apart and break the spell that had washed over them.

But at last they did draw apart, only to lay entwined with her head on his shoulder, one of his legs across her thigh in a protective gesture. Maddie's throat felt thick with tears. She didn't know why she was so close to crying, except that no experience—no *person*—had ever moved her quite so much. She squeezed her eyes shut and breathed in deeply of the scent of him—male musk and sex mingled with the faint sweetness of chocolate and the comforting aroma of clean sheets.

The thought occurred to her that one of the worst nights of her life was also turning out to be one of her best. She couldn't change the opinion of people such as that reporter who saw her as a failure. She couldn't turn back time and stop herself from hurtling down that slope with such reckless abandon.

But she could lie here in the arms of a man about whom she cared deeply and savor the moment. She didn't dare tell Hagan of her feelings—those words were guaranteed to make him panic. He was a man who had stopped believing in the possibility of happily-ever-after.

She wasn't too sure herself if such fairy tales were possible, but she was certain that Hagan had given her a very special gift tonight—one that had nothing to do with sex and everything to do with trust and friendship and a willingness to risk himself, or at least his privacy, on her behalf. He hadn't physically injured Randy, as he'd offered, but his anger on her behalf had struck a blow to the hurt she'd carried away from that viewing party.

And here in his arms, for this moment at least, she could believe that one day people like Randy wouldn't have the power to hurt her, that Hagan's faith and caring had given her a shield against ugly words and uglier memories.

Chapter Thirteen

Maddie woke early the next morning to Hagan's hand on her shoulder, gently shaking her. "We have to hurry," he said. "We overslept."

He was already dressed in his ski patrol uniform, and he moved about the room, collecting gear. "I have to be on the mountain at seven for avalanche control," he said. "I'll drop you off at your place on the way."

"All right." She started to get out of bed, then realized she was naked beneath the covers. Shyness overwhelmed her. Last night she had thought nothing of showing herself to him, but last night had been a romantic dream. This morning the atmosphere was one of cold practicality, with no good-morning kisses or cuddling, only Hagan in his uniform, all business.

"Could you toss me my clothes?" she asked, trying to sound as unconcerned as he.

He did as she asked. "I have coffee and toast downstairs when you are ready," he said, then left.

She dressed quickly, made use of the bathroom, running his brush through her hair, borrowing his toothpaste to scrub over her teeth with a finger. She felt the intimacy of being here in this most private space, yet a strange disconnectedness, too, as if the events of last night had never taken place.

She came downstairs and poured a cup of coffee. Hagan passed her, loaded down with skis, boots and backpack. "I will warm up the truck. Come out whenever you are ready."

So this was how it was to be. No good-morning kiss. No murmured endearments. She wanted to demand better of him, but then, he had promised no more than one night, and it seemed he intended to keep that promise.

She shrugged into her coat and gloves and carried her mug of coffee out to the truck and climbed in. She balanced the coffee mug on the dash and reached around to fasten the seat belt, then felt his hand on her arm.

"I want to kiss you now," he said. "You will not want me to do it at your condo, where someone might see and talk."

Which she translated to mean *he* didn't want to be seen or talked about, but she was relieved to enjoy at least this sign of affection.

It was no perfunctory kiss, either, but a lingering, full-mouth celebration of a kiss, full of heat and tenderness…and the promise of more. When at last he broke away, he did so reluctantly, and his eyes held a definite message of *to be continued.*

Maddie was not at her best early in the morning and Hagan seemed disinclined to talk, so the drive back to town passed in silence. He stopped the truck briefly in front of her condos. "See you in a little while," he said by way of goodbye, then drove away.

Maddie tried to slip into the condo without making any noise, but Andrea was already awake and in the kitchen. "Where have *you* been all night?" Andrea asked. "I've been wondering how long I should wait to file a missing persons report."

"Why would you do that?" Maddie took off her coat and draped it over the back of a chair. "Is there any more coffee?"

"There's plenty." She moved aside to allow Maddie access to the coffeemaker. "You can't blame me for worrying, after the way you ran out of the conference room yesterday evening. I thought you'd come back here, but when you didn't, I started calling people. No one had seen you after you left. You'd disappeared."

"I'm sorry. I didn't mean to worry you." Maddie poured coffee and added cream. "I stayed with a friend."

"A friend?" Andrea eyed her skeptically. "Someone I don't know?"

Maddie took her time stirring her cup. It wasn't that she didn't want Andrea to know about Hagan, but until she knew where this—whatever it was between them— was going, she felt better keeping quiet. If it truly had been only one night, she'd rather not expose either of them to gossip. "Maybe I'll tell you later, but I can't now," she said with a pleading look.

Andrea looked at her a moment longer, then sighed. "All right. I guess you're entitled to your privacy."

Maddie leaned against the kitchen counter and sipped her coffee. "What happened last night after I left?" she asked.

"We watched the rest of the interview. There

wasn't much. I thought that reporter talked to you for an hour or more."

"He did. How much made it onto the show?"

"About five minutes." Andrea put her empty cereal bowl in the sink. "The rat."

Maddie laughed. Already the events of the night before seemed distant and of lesser importance. Her friends would be busy with the Free Skiing Championship. Plus Zephyr's event was today and no matter what the outcome of his competition, there would be celebrating tonight.

And eventually, she would see Hagan again. The idea sent a pleasant flutter through her, even as she reminded herself that there was no certainty he'd want to pick up where they'd left off last night. She believed he truly cared for her, but the very fact of his caring made him wary. She could repeatedly tell him she would never hurt him the way his ex-wife had, but there were no iron-clad guarantees in life, as she knew too well.

She and Andrea dressed, gathered their gear, and caught the shuttle to the resort. Already crowds were gathering. Andrea headed for the extreme terrain to help with the events, while Maddie was assigned to patrol the more populated green, blue and black runs. She had never formally requested this assignment, but somehow the message had been communicated to keep her away from the extreme territory unless absolutely necessary. The knowledge grated, even though she appreciated the consideration.

She had a typical morning: retrieving a dropped ski pole from beneath the Silver Queen lift, reuniting a lost child with his father, transporting a teen with a broken wrist from the terrain park to the clinic. Gone was the disdain for such tasks that had filled her during her early days on the job. Now she enjoyed most of her encounters with visitors, and took pride in her ability to do her job well. No one would award her a medal at the end of a day's work, but she'd found something here that she had grown to value even more: a sense of belonging, and of being accepted, even loved.

She still missed racing and competing, but, last night's cruel reminder aside, she no longer agonized over what might have been. The long-awaited inner healing everyone had promised had finally begun. She'd lost her old dream, but she was starting to believe in the possibility of finding a new one.

Proof was in the fact that, while she enjoyed meeting and talking with the athletes competing in the Free Skiing events, she no longer saw herself as one of them. She wasn't a transient stopping only long enough to ski a few runs, but one of the locals who welcomed guests with a slight smugness that she got to stay in this beautiful place after they'd moved on. That feeling alone told her how far she'd come from her earlier bitterness.

The only jarring note in the otherwise pleasant day were the occasional messages that came across the radio regarding some participant in the Free Skiing events needing transport to the clinic, and once, an ambulance left the area, sirens screaming. Reminders of the real danger behind all the fun.

Maddie found herself watching for Hagan, but never saw him. Just as well. She feared one look at him and she'd give herself away; even thinking of him was enough to put a goofy smile on her face. She only wished she could be sure she had the same effect on him.

HAGAN AND SCOTT HANDED the stretcher off to the EMT then headed up the lift to return to the competition. "That's number six today," Scott said. "Not bad for an event like this."

"None of them have been too serious," Hagan said. One dislocated shoulder, a couple of twisted knees, one possible arm fracture and some miscellaneous bumps and bruises. Nothing life-threatening or potentially career-ending.

"Yeah. I guess when you're leaping off twenty-foot cliffs and flying around rocks and trees, injuries come with the territory," Scott said. "Let's hope we get through the rest of the day without anything major."

Hagan nodded. Patrollers trained hard for the worst-case scenario, then hoped to never have to put that training into practice. "What is up next?" he asked.

Scott pulled a paper schedule from his pocket and scanned it. "Snowboarders."

"I have a friend in this event."

"Fine by me if you take a break and watch."

Hagan hiked to the area where the snowboarding event was to take place the same location where he and Zephyr had practiced. He found Zephyr, dressed in orange-and-black camo-patterned pants and an orange jacket. "Afraid people will miss you?" Hagan asked.

Zephyr grinned. "No sense blending in with the scenery."

"Good luck." Hagan clapped his friend on the back,

then moved over to the side. The terrain was not built for spectators. The best he could hope for was to watch Zephyr's takeoff and wait with everyone else for the results to come through over the radio.

Meanwhile, there were at least three other boarders who would make their runs before Zephyr, and lots of time to wait.

Time in which Hagan's thoughts were pulled away from the activity on the slope, to last night with Maddie. The whole evening had had a dreamlike quality, from the moment he found her at the bus stop until he had fallen asleep beside her in his bed, as if some other man had taken over his body for a while. A man for whom caution and consequences had no meaning. Someone for whom love was as simple as a lingering kiss and as uncomplicated as a night of uninhibited passion with a woman who meant the world to him.

The knowledge of how much Maddie had come to mean to him made it difficult to breathe. That kind of caring was a guarantee of pain later. Not that he believed she had any intention of hurting him. Not now. But that was the way life worked—things happened, people changed, and all the love in the world could not stop it. Not in his experience anyway. The only way to avoid the hurt was to avoid getting too deeply involved. It was a defense that had worked for him so far.

Until Maddie. Against her it seemed he had no defenses at all. He was not a man who was afraid of much, but the idea that she had ensnared him so completely made him shiver. He had to find a graceful way out of this. One that would keep both of them from getting in any deeper. One that would lessen the injuries. Last night had been truly special, but better to keep that wonderful memory intact than to let the vagaries of real life tarnish it.

SOMEONE HAD DRAGGED the big-screen television into the cafeteria and tuned it to ESPN's coverage of the Free Skiing Championship. Word had circulated when it was time for Zephyr's event and Maddie, Andrea and others had gathered to watch.

"Awesome camera work," Max said as they watched a snowboarder sail off a snowy cornice and make a perfect landing in the thick powder below. "Up on the mountain, you really can't see anything."

"I feel sick." Trish held her stomach and leaned forward in her chair as the snowboarder on the screen hurtled down a slope that looked nearly vertical. "That looks so dangerous."

"It's a wicked line," Patti offered. "But these guys know what they're doing."

"Zephyr never knows what he's doing," Trish said. "You know how he is. The original space cadet."

"He comes across as a flake, but he's a pro on his board," Max said. "And he's been practicing. He's ready for this."

Trish clenched her fists in her lap. "I don't know why I'm even here," she said. "I ought to go back to the shop. He'll show up there later to tell me all about it anyway." But she made no move to leave.

"Look, there's Zephyr!" Casey pointed at the screen to a familiar figure, the ends of his dreadlocks sticking out from beneath his gray helmet. He was dressed in loud orange and black.

"Where did he get the threads?" Patti asked.

"Special order," Max said. "He wanted to stand out in a crowd."

"He certainly does that," Maddie said.

Zephyr took his position at the top of the run. Maddie bit her lip, surprised at how tense she was. Maybe because she knew better than most the danger of what he was about to do. She knew how steep and narrow the run was, and knew all the things that could go wrong.

"There he goes," Max shouted, as Zephyr took off down the run. He sped down the first stretch and entered the trees, cutting a tight line in and out.

"Look at him go," Max said. "He's rocking and rolling now."

Even Trish was smiling. "He looks amazing up there."

He took the first jump, made a showy grab and an arms-up landing that drew cheers from the crowd on the slope and in the cafeteria. Maddie leaned forward, intent on the screen, marveling at the turns Zephyr executed with seeming ease.

"I had no idea he was this good," Trish breathed. She was smiling, her cheeks flushed pink.

The next section of the run was a line of steep cliffs. Zephyr poised at the top of one, surveying his line. The camera panned in close, showing the distance to a safe landing. The route required one fifteen-foot jump to another section of cliffs, a sharp right turn and a second ten-foot jump. The announcer murmured something about the degree of difficulty, and then Zephyr was airborne.

Maddie held her breath as he floated down, bright orange against the pristine snow and dark trees. He landed in a fountain of snow, obscured in a cloud for a moment, then rocketed out.

More cheers went up, louder this time, but celebration turned to horror as Maddie realized Zephyr was traveling much too fast. Something was wrong. His stance was off, then his board was hurtling one direction, Zephyr another.

She groaned out loud when he hit the tree, and stared, unbelieving, at the crumpled orange figure prone in the snow.

"What happened?" Trish asked. She rose from her chair. "Is he all right? What's going on?"

No one answered. No one even looked at her. They stared at the television screen, as the camera zoomed in closer. Zephyr's face was turned away from them, only the side of his helmet and part of one cheek visible. He was curled against the tree trunk. And he wasn't moving.

THE FIRST CLUE Hagan had that something was wrong was a wave of murmuring that traveled up the slope from the spectators farther down. Hagan only caught snatches of phrases such as "didn't stick the landing" and "looks bad."

Just then, his radio crackled. Scott's voice was tense. "Hagan, we need you down here above the cliffs on Body Bag."

His stomach lurched, and he did not bother asking who was injured or to what extent. Every second counted with a serious injury, and he immediately started down the run, ignoring the shouted questions of those around him.

Scott met him in the trees above the cliffs where Zephyr would have made his second jump. "He came off the edge, made what looked like a good landing, then lost it and slammed into a tree," Scott said, pointing down the chute. "Looks like his binding might have broken, but we're not sure."

Hagan edged as far as he dared onto the cornice and peered over. He could barely make out the crumpled orange figure below. "Zephyr!" he shouted.

"We've been shouting to him, not getting a response." Scott nodded to Eric and one of the ESPN cameramen who had joined them. "Could be a head injury or a spinal cord trauma or anything."

"We will have to rope down to him," Hagan said. He clicked out of his skis and shoved them into the snow at one side. "We have gear stashed somewhere around here, do we not?"

Scott put out his arm. "Hold on. You're not going."

"I am the most experienced climber," Hagan said.

"And one of the biggest guys on patrol." Still holding his arm, Scott pointed down once more. "See that cornice he's on? It's about eight feet wide and brittle as hell. We get some big guy down there stomping around it's liable to shear off and then you'll both be in trouble."

"So what are you going to do?" the cameraman asked.

Scott frowned at him. Hagan knew he did not like having an outsider in on the discussion, but they would waste precious time arguing over the matter. "I've radioed for Maddie. She's the smallest and lightest, and she told me she skied this area with you and Zephyr a few weeks ago. We can either rope her up and send her down, or she could probably ski a tight line to him."

He indicated a skinny strip of snow arcing onto the cornice. "She'll have to assess the injuries, stabilize him the best she can and lower him in a harness."

Hagan did not even realize he had been shaking his head until Scott stopped and looked at him. "What's wrong with the plan?"

"Do not ask Maddie. Get Andrea or one of the other women." If Maddie had had a hard time over here the other day, what would it be like for her now—after the replay of her own accident last night, with all these people and television cameras around? And even worse than if she lost her nerve, what if she fell and was hurt? He felt physically ill at the thought and sucked in a deep breath, trying to clear his head.

"She's already on her way," Scott said. He turned to Eric. "I want you and Hagan to take a toboggan down under the cliff and be ready to get Zephyr to the bottom of Body Bag. Marcie will be there with a snowmobile and get him to either an ambulance or Life Flight waiting at the parking lot."

Hagan shouldered his skis and began climbing up with Eric. He wanted to protest further—not only for Maddie's sake but for Zephyr's. If she freaked out, it would delay getting help to the injured snowboarder. But Scott was firm with this plan and time was passing.

All Hagan could do was watch for the chance to intercept her before she reached Scott and convince her to refuse the assignment. For everyone's peace of mind, including his own.

SEEING ZEPHYR FALL kickstarted Maddie's visceral memory of her own accident—the triumphant sensation of speed, the knowledge that she was winning the race, then the split-second horror at losing control, the shock of the first impact, then the blackness of nothing, moments that were lost to her forever, mercifully blotted out in the months of pain and fear that followed.

She was moving toward the door of the cafeteria before she even realized it, already planning how she would get to Zephyr. She, more than anyone, might be able to help him.

The loud crackle of her radio barely cut through the fog in which she traveled. She answered it automatically, still moving toward her skis. "Maddie, this is Scott. We need you up here on Body Bag. I'm sending a sled for you."

She looked up and saw the snowmobile headed straight down the slope. She ran out to meet it and was stashing her skis in back before Marcie had even slowed the machine. "Hold on," Marcie called over her shoulder. "We're in a hurry here."

The snowmobile flew over the slopes, siren wailing. Maddie clutched Marcie's shoulders, her whole body tensed, wondering what they would find on the macabrely name Body Bag.

Marcie radioed when they reached the staging area for the race. "I want Maddie to ski to me above the cliffs on Body Bag," Scott said. "You take the sled to where the run empties out and wait for Hagan and Eric to bring the toboggan."

Maddie was already into her skis, adrenaline making her muscles twitch as she tightened her boots and reached for her ski poles. She scarcely thought of the steepness of the slope today, all her attention was on what lay ahead. How would they get to Zephyr? How badly was he hurt? How would they get him off that cliff?

Then Hagan was beside her. A sense of great relief welled up in her at the sight of him. Having him here made everything better. "What's going on?" she asked. "How's Zephyr?"

He shook his head. "He is not responding to our shouts, but we have no way of knowing the extent of his injuries." Worry lines creased his forehead and radiated from his eyes. "He is stuck on a cornice. Scott wants you to ski or climb down, get him into a harness then lower him down to a toboggan."

She nodded. "I can do that."

Hagan grabbed her arm. "You do not have to do this," he said. "Let Andrea or someone else go."

She frowned. "Why shouldn't I go?"

"It is a bad area. Narrow and steep. The most expert skier would think twice about attempting it."

"And you think I'll freak out." Although she knew he was looking out for her, his lack of confidence in her stung—a lot.

His expression softened. "You do not have to prove anything to anyone. After what you have been through, you have a right to refuse to go."

She looked down the slope, and pictured the rocks and chutes ahead. Worse than anything she'd encountered on a race course. "Why did Scott pick me for the job?"

Hagan hesitated, then said, "You are the lightest and smallest patroller. The cornice will not support much weight."

She took a deep breath and nodded: "Then I have to go."

"Maddie—"

She shook off his hand and planted her ski poles in front of her. "I have to do this. I'm tired of living as a coward."

Not waiting for an answer, she started down the run. Her heart hammered in her chest, and she felt cold from the inside out. But she wouldn't let that stop her. She had to help Zephyr—and in doing so, maybe help herself.

Maddie was surprised at how quickly she reached Scott. She'd skied automatically, not thinking about the incline or slickness of the run.

But standing in these cliffs and trees was a different story. She looked down on the impossible line Scott wanted her to ski to reach the cornice and felt faint. "We can rope you up and send you over the cliff," he said. "But skiing will be faster and we don't know how badly he's hurt." *Or how much time we have to save him* was the unspoken end of the sentence.

All her emergency responder training cut through her panicked thoughts, fragments of textbooks and quotes from lecturers: *In the case of cervical fracture, it is crucial that treatment be initiated immediately. Delay may increase the chances of paralysis or even death.*

If the patient is unresponsive and not breathing, mouth-to-mouth resuscitation should begin immediately. Any delay increases the risk of serious disability or death.

She swallowed hard and nodded. "I'll do my best," she said.

"You'll need this." Scott picked up a portable oxygen cylinder and mask and motioned for her to turn around so he could attach it to her pack, which already contained a supply of braces, splints, bandages and other first aid materials. "We'll lower a backboard and harness to you once you've assessed the situation," he said.

She nodded, mute. Gut-churning fear had stolen her voice.

"Maddie?"

She forced herself to raise her head, to meet Scott's eyes. "You can do this," he said. "It's a tight line, but it's short. I'm not asking for perfect. Skid down the thing if you have to. Just get down it."

She nodded. "I'll do it." She would find a way. Her own fear didn't matter right now. She was doing this for Zephyr. She was the only one who could help him. She couldn't afford to fail.

Chapter Fourteen

Maddie knew if she studied her route too long the fear would get the upper hand, so she planted her pole and headed down, wrenching around the first turn, skidding sharply but managing to stay upright. The fronts of her skis scraped rocks as she continued down and she knew she was leaning back too far. Leaning forward at that angle—surely it was a fifty percent slope—was terrifying, but she knew she had to do it.

Bending her knees, she hunched forward and reached her pole into the next turn. Again she skidded and struggled to stay on the band of icy snow. She felt dizzy, and forced herself to breathe deeply. Only fifty more feet to go, straight down, then a sharp right turn to the edge of the cornice.

As soon as she reached the ledge, she kicked out of her skis and knelt beside Zephyr. She touched his shoulder gently and he groaned. She had never welcomed a sound of pain as much. "He's alive!" she shouted, and a cheer went up from those above and below.

"Zephyr, it's Maddie," she said, slipping off her pack and opening it beside him. "What's going on?"

"Hey." He offered a weak smile and tried to roll over onto his back, but she stopped him.

"Don't move," she said. "Tell me where it hurts."

"Easier…to say…where it…doesn't."

She looked at his legs. The right one stuck out at an odd angle, but when she probed it, she felt no exposed bone. "Can you move your feet?" she asked. "Wiggle your toes for me."

He did as she asked, but winced. "Right knee's banged up," he said. "And my shoulder and arm."

But no spinal cord injury. No blood that she could see. Things were looking better all the time. "All right," she said, checking his pulse, which was rapid, but strong. "I'm going to get you stabilized, then you're going to go for a little ride."

As HAGAN WATCHED Maddie ski to where Zephyr lay, her last words echoed in his head. *I'm tired of living as a coward.*

He knew how terrifying this was for her, yet she forced herself to do it anyway. He admired that determination. When was the last time he had risked anything on behalf of someone else—not only physical risk, but emotional? He had been so resolved not to be hurt again he had not allowed himself to feel much of anything.

Until Maddie. Maddie had made him feel a hundred things, from self-loathing to surprise to the potential of love. But that potential could only become real if he was willing to take a risk.

"Come on." Eric slapped him on the back. "Let's get that toboggan down there."

The plastic rescue sled was stationed in the trees

beneath the cliffs. Hagan and Eric climbed down to it, unfastened it from its mooring and wrestled the toboggan into position beneath the cliff. "It's going to be a bitch to get it down from here," Eric said, looking at the slope below.

Hagan nodded. "Do you want head or tail?"

"I'll take the rear, I guess." Eric would act as an extra brake on the rear, and also serve as a visual monitor on Zephyr.

But first they had to get Zephyr loaded.

From where he stood, Hagan could just see Maddie working. Occasionally the murmur of her voice drifted down to him, not distinct words, but the soothing tone and gentle cadence.

Last night he had fallen asleep with the memory of her voice—her murmured endearments and cries of pleasure. He had awakened smiling, and had only to turn his head to look at her, asleep on the pillow beside him, to know why.

He had made a practice of never letting any woman touch him deeply. He had enjoyed their company and done his best to make sure they enjoyed his, but had never gone beneath the surface of any emotion.

And in one night Maddie had buried herself deeply inside him, so that her scent, her voice, her touch were already a part of him.

She was standing now, reaching for the harness into which she would fasten Zephyr. Eric and Hagan readied to receive him. "I've stabilized his shoulder and splinted his right knee, leg and arm and taped the arm to his body," she radioed. "And I've administered oxygen and pain medication."

She had made Zephyr as comfortable as she could. Now it was their turn.

Working silently, the two men lowered their patient to the ground and lifted him into the toboggan. "How are you doing?" Hagan asked.

Zephyr gave them a goofy smile. "It was gnarly for a while, but I'm better now."

"Could I have a few words with him?" The ESPN reporter and cameraman moved forward.

Hagan glared at them. "No. Get back."

Either his intimidating stance or the tone of his voice cowed them; they moved off into the trees, though the camera still recorded.

Zephyr groaned.

Hagan knelt beside him. "What is it?" he asked. "Is something wrong?"

"Was that the media?" Zephyr peered at him from the cocoon of blankets in which they had wrapped him. "Have they been filming this?"

"'Fraid so, dude," Eric said. "But think of it this way. You'll be famous. They'll be replaying your crash all over the country."

"Then I guess Trish saw it," Zephyr muttered as his eyes drifted closed.

"Dude, everybody saw it," Eric said. "Like I said, you're gonna be famous."

Maddie would probably argue that was a fame no one really wanted, but Hagan said nothing, merely stepped between the handles of the toboggan. "Ready?" he called over his shoulder.

"Ready," Eric said, and they started down.

MADDIE COLLECTED HER SKIS and climbed down, too spent to risk negotiating the narrow chutes and sharp turns. When she reached the bottom, she clicked into her skis and followed the path Hagan and Eric had left, hoping to make her way quickly to the base and get an update on Zephyr's condition.

But at the bottom her progress was blocked by Randy Milligan. He held a microphone and behind him stood a cameraman. "That was a spectacular rescue up there," he said. "What were you thinking when you skied down to the injured snowboarder?"

She stared at him, any number of sarcastic answers poised on the tip of her tongue. But facing a reporter was like facing a criminal charge—anything she said could and would be used against her. "I was thinking about the boarder, what injuries I might encounter and how best to treat them," she answered.

"What went wrong to cause this to happen?" he asked.

A question she'd asked herself after her own accident. And finally, she had the right answer, the one that had eluded her for so long. "It was just an accident. No one plans for these things to happen. It's part of the risk in this sport. Taking chances is a requirement to be good and part of the reason this is so exciting."

The very recklessness that had helped her climb to the top of the standings on the World Cup Tour had eventually been her downfall but she'd finally realized—as she'd tended to Zephyr's injuries—that caution wouldn't have necessarily kept her safer, and it certainly wouldn't have helped her win as many races as she had. What had happened hadn't been entirely her fault, and it was time she stopped beating herself up about it.

"Given your own history of skiing injuries, were you in doubt about your ability to ski down to the cornice?" Randy shoved the microphone closer. "It's a very risky route."

"I wasn't thinking about myself. I was thinking about Zephyr."

"That's the boarder's name, is it? Just Zephyr? No last name?"

"I have to go."

She tried to push past them, but Randy stepped in front of her once more. "Just a few more questions. You looked very tentative up at the top of the slope. Were you reliving your own accident as you stood up there? Or remembering other times when you'd attempted a challenging run and balked?"

She told herself she showed remarkable restraint in not answering his questions, but the truth was she could think of nothing to say. He'd pegged her a failure and wouldn't let go of that label no matter what she said or did. But it didn't matter what he thought. She wasn't a public figure anymore—her reputation was no longer shaped by what others thought of her. All that mattered was her own opinion, and those of the people close to her. People who cared about her for more than the medals she won or how good she looked racing down a slope. "I have to go see to my friend," she said, then threw out one elbow and almost knocked him over as she skied past.

She arrived at the base area in time to see the helicopter disappearing from view over the horizon. She stood watching it, glad Zephyr would reach a hospital quickly. She prayed there weren't other, unseen internal injuries to deal with—the broken bones would be plenty.

Trish rushed to her. Her face was pale and her eyes puffy, as if she'd been crying. "How is he?" she asked, clutching at Maddie's arm. "They wouldn't tell me anything."

Max and Casey joined them, their faces full of concern. "He's going to be all right," Maddie said. "He has some injuries—maybe a broken bone or two—but he was talking and in good shape, considering."

"He looked so awful, lying there." Trish bit her lip.

"It was a pretty horrendous fall," Max said. "And then the camera focused in on him, just lying there, for a long time."

"I think he probably had the breath knocked out of him, or he may even have lost consciousness for a little bit. By the time I got to him, he was able to talk." She patted Trish's shoulder. "He's going to be all right. I'm sure of it."

"That was awesome, what you did," Max said. "They showed it on TV. I don't think I could have gotten down to him."

"It wasn't so bad," she said. Not something she'd do every day, but if she had to do it again to help another injured person, she was confident she could. The reward of helping someone, the rush of good feeling, was better than any medal she'd ever won. She'd never imagined it could feel that way.

"I'm going to the hospital," Trish said. "They'll have taken him to Gunnison, won't they?"

"I'm not sure," Maddie admitted.

"We'll find out." Max put his arm around Trish. "Come on, we'll go with you."

Casey waved and followed them toward the parking lot. Maddie turned and was heading for the locker room when Hagan hailed her.

"I have to get back to the competition," he said, jogging over to her. "Are you okay?"

The concern in his eyes made her heart flip over. The impact of all she'd been through in the last hour hit her and she suddenly felt weak. She wanted to throw her arms around him and let him hold her for a while, drawing on his strength.

But of course, she couldn't do that. They each had jobs to do, and if Hagan hadn't wanted to kiss her goodbye this morning in the almost empty parking lot of her condo, he certainly wouldn't want to embrace her here in the middle of this busy ski resort.

"I'm okay," she said instead, offering him a wobbly smile. "Tired, but happy Zephyr is going to be all right."

He put a hand on her shoulder, his eyes still locked to hers. She could have fallen into that gaze, abandoned work and responsibility and everything to all they promised. "What you did back there," he said, "that was really brave."

Coming down that strip of snow and ice, she'd felt terrified, desperate, even unsure of her sanity, but never brave. "I had to do it," she said. "There wasn't anyone else."

"Not everyone would have done it." His radio crackled, and he slid his hand away. She had to bite her lip to keep from crying out for him to stay. "I have to go," he said.

He started to move away, then turned back and pulled her close. She scarcely had time to register his arms around her before his mouth was on hers.

It was a kiss full of passion and promise, and an almost desperate longing that made tears sting behind her tightly closed eyelids. He held her so tightly her ribs might have cracked, but she scarcely noticed, too caught up in joy and the knowledge that he loved her. He'd never said the words, but this kiss said it better than any muttered syllables. Fear, admiration, relief—the kiss communicated all those emotions and more. But none of them would have been there without love.

She was still light-headed when he reluctantly released her and turned away. Only as she stared after his retreating back did she come to her senses enough to realize that everyone around her was staring, wide-eyed and openmouthed. Andrea, Patti, Lisa—almost everyone they knew here at the resort and in town. Hagan must have known they were there. She couldn't contain her smile, even as she blinked back fresh tears. That hadn't only been a kiss Hagan had given her—he had made a public statement of his feelings.

Whether he realized it or not.

BY THE END OF THE DAY, Hagan was exhausted. There had been no other serious injuries in the afternoon's competition, but the adrenaline rush of Zephyr's rescue had sapped everything from him. The parking lot seemed miles away and when he finally reached his truck, he sat for a while with his hands on the steering wheel, staring at nothing, mustering the strength to drive home.

He would feel better after a shower, he told himself as he started the engine and turned the vehicle toward the highway. He would clean up, change clothes and grab something to eat. Then maybe he would pick up Maddie and they could drive to the hospital to see Zephyr.

But when he turned onto the drive to his cabin, he was surprised to see a red Outback parked beneath the trees beside the house. While he was trying to remember where he had seen the car before, his front door opened and Maddie stepped out.

"I hope you don't mind," she said, walking out to meet him. "I wanted to talk to you when there weren't a lot of people around."

She had changed into a form-fitting red sweater that came down over her hips and black leggings stuffed into fur-trimmed boots. It was a sexy outfit that left no doubt about her shapely figure but then, the memory of her shape was already firmly fixed in his mind, so that if she had swathed herself in padded down she would still turn him on. "I do not mind," he said, reaching behind to retrieve his backpack, giving himself time to regain his composure.

She helped him carry his gear inside, but as soon as the door closed behind him she wrapped her arms around him and gave him a long, deep kiss. The kind of kiss that made a man forget his name. It certainly made him forget all about being tired. He smoothed his hands down her hips and tugged her body closer to his, debating whether to invite her into the shower with him or take her straight to bed.

But then she slipped out of his arms, a half smile on

her lips, and moved to the sofa. "We need to talk about a few things," she said.

Dangerous words from any woman, but he felt no fear now, only curiosity. And indeed, he had a lot he wanted to say to her, if he could only find the words.

He sat beside her, but she did not look at him. Her gaze darted from the fire to the skis over the door, to the door itself, as if she was fighting a sudden urge to leave. After the bold kiss at the door, he found her discomfort charming. He sat back and waited, saying nothing.

She took a deep breath and squared her shoulders, then turned and fixed her gaze on him at last. "I'm not very good at pretending or playing games, so I came here to confess that this 'just one night, no promises, no strings' relationship isn't going to work for me. I'm sorry. I wanted to give it a try, but I'm not made that way."

He stared at her, not blinking, not breathing. If possible, his heart had stopped beating. Was she breaking up with him? Is this what he got for letting himself think he could trust his feelings and try a long-term relationship again? But he had to say something. She was staring at him. He opened his mouth. "I see," he said, in a strange, croaking voice.

"You were honest with me, so I'm trying to be honest with you," she said, sounding much calmer now that she had dropped her verbal bomb. "I know you've had lots of practice with this sort of thing, but I'm not cut out for it. I guess I'm an all-or-nothing sort of woman."

He sat up straighter, keeping his face expressionless. One thing he *would not* do was let her see how much she had devastated him. "So you are saying goodbye."

Her own pleasant expression crumbled. "Goodbye? Is that what you want?"

"Is that not what you want?"

"Why would you think that?"

He kept his gaze focused on the coffee table. On the pile of books in the middle of it. "You said this relationship was not working out for you."

He did not even see the missile coming. When the pillow bounced off his head, he blinked, then stared at her. "What are you doing?" he asked.

"I'm trying to knock some sense into you!" She stood and began pacing back and forth, arms gesturing, head tossing, as if simple words were not enough to convey her true emotions. "Hagan Ansdar, do you or do you not love me?"

It was his turn to be stunned—he did not even try to hide it. "Yes," he said. He cleared his throat. "Yes, I love you."

She nodded. "Good. I love you, too. So you agree that we've got more than a one-night stand going on here? That short-term isn't going to cut it for us?"

He nodded again, a man in a dream—a strange dream where he could not quite follow the plotline. "I had definitely hoped for more than short term."

She dropped down onto the sofa beside him once more. "Then don't scare me with talk of goodbye."

He collapsed against the cushions once more, regarding her warily. "You are the one who started talking about things not working out. What was I supposed to think?"

She gave him an exasperated look. "You were supposed to agree with me."

He nodded. "My father once said that was the best approach to dealing with women."

He dodged the pillow this time, and pulled her into his arms. Kissing her was the only sure way he knew of silencing her, and she seemed agreeable, spending a long time with her arms around him, eventually sliding over to sit in his lap. "I love you, Hagan," she said again.

"I love you, too." He looked into her eyes, something he hoped he never tired of doing. She had beautiful eyes, a rich brown color, like coffee laced with Baileys. "I never thought I would say that to a woman again."

"And I never thought I'd fall for a man who was such a player."

He put a finger to her lips. "Never again. I promise. As long as we are together, you are the only woman I want to be with."

"I see you're still hedging your bets," she teased.

He frowned. "I do not know if I believe anything lasts forever, but for you, I will try."

She smiled. "That's all I ask. We'll try together. We'll get to forever—one day at a time."

"And one night at a time." He bent his lips to hers once more. "Do not forget the nights."

It was a long while before they broke apart. "Are you too tired to drive to the hospital tonight?" she asked. "I'd really like to check on Zephyr."

"We will go." He patted her thigh. "Let me take a shower and eat something first." He quirked an eyebrow at her. "Or, you could help with the shower."

She laughed. "If I do that, we won't make it to the hospital tonight." She stood. "I'll fix some food while you shower."

AN HOUR LATER, Maddie and Hagan entered Zephyr's room at Gunnison Valley Hospital. Though her euphoria over Hagan's declaration of love had blotted out some of her worry about their friend, now that they were here she looked anxiously toward the inert figure in the bed.

Trish smiled at them from her bedside seat. "Hey, guys," she said.

"How is he?" Hagan asked.

"They've got him doped up pretty good." Trish's grin widened and she brushed the hair back from Zephyr's forehead. "Of course with him, it's sometimes hard to tell."

Zephyr opened his eyes and stared at them owlishly. "Hey," he said, offering a crooked smile.

"They operated to put a pin in his leg," Trish said. "His arm is in a cast and he'll probably need surgery on his knee when the swelling goes down. And his shoulder was dislocated, but they put it back into place."

Maddie winced at this list of injuries, but—perhaps thanks to whatever painkillers the doctors had administered—Zephyr was taking them in stride. "If I'd tried harder, I probably could have broken a few more bones," he offered.

"Idiot," Trish said without a hint of malice. She offered him a cup of water with a straw and he sipped. She glanced back at Maddie and Hagan. "I'm hoping I've talked him out of any more Free Skiing competitions. I don't think my heart can take it, even if his can."

"No, I'm done with that," Zephyr said, waving the hand that held his IV. "I'm moving on to something better."

"Better?" Maddie moved closer. "What's that?"

His grin broadened. "Television!"

"Television?" Trish looked doubtful.

"I'm a nat'ral," he slurred, closing his eyes. "You watch. I'll be great at it."

She shook her head and tucked the covers more securely around him. "It's a good thing my coffee shop makes enough to support both of us."

Hagan and Maddie said good-night. When they left the room, Trish was still gazing at Zephyr fondly. "There is an unlikely pair," Hagan said as he and Maddie walked toward the elevator.

"Oh, I don't know," Maddie said. "I think Trish is the type of woman who likes to look after other people. And Zephyr certainly needs someone to look after him. He might even help her discover her dreamier side." She looked up at him. "Then again, maybe the two of them just clicked. It happens sometimes."

He slipped his arm around her. "Yes. I guess it does."

Clicking was as good a description as any Maddie could come up with to explain why she, out of all the women Hagan had known, had captured his heart. And the only reason she could fathom why she had fallen for a man who, on the surface at least, had seemed so wrong for her.

"What are your plans for this summer?" he asked when they reached his truck.

It was a question she'd given a lot of thought to lately, not only because of her growing attachment to Hagan, but because of the need to decide what kind of future she would build for herself. Up there on that ledge with Zephyr, she'd finally let go of the last bit of pain over losing her old dream, and had cleared the way to search for a new dream. "I want to stay in Crested Butte," she said, fastening her seat belt. "But I'll need to find a job and a new place to live, since the condo is part of the job and when the job ends, so does my stay there."

"You should try the forest service. I can get you on as a seasonal ranger."

She shook her head. "Thanks, but I had something else in mind." An idea had taken hold of her this afternoon, its appeal growing the more she contemplated it. "I think I'd like to study to be a paramedic. Full certification. And I'd like to try to hire on with Emergency Services in Gunnison."

"What brought this on?"

"I guess it's been in the back of my mind for a while," she said. "You remember I told you I joined ski patrol as a way to pay back all the people who helped me recover from my injuries?"

He nodded.

She turned toward him, the excitement of sharing her plans growing. "This afternoon, when I was taking care of Zephyr, it was such an incredible feeling, knowing I was helping him. I never felt like that before. It was better than winning a medal." She hugged herself, reliving that moment of triumph there in those snowy cliffs. "I realized *this* was what I wanted to do with my life. *This* was the goal I'd been missing."

He reached over and patted her leg. "You will be a great EMT," he said.

She covered his hand her hers. "I want to be. It's the first thing I've really wanted since my accident."

He took his hand from her and started the engine,

then glanced at her. "You will still need a place to live," he said. "I know a cabin that definitely has room for two."

The offhand manner in which he delivered this invitation amused her. Hagan would never be a man to wear his heart on his sleeve. Which made the brief instances when he let down his guard all the more meaningful.

But she would never be one to let him off easy. Just as she'd forced his hand by going to his cabin this evening, she wasn't afraid to do so again.

"The offer is tempting," she said, gazing out the windshield with her own imitation of indifference. "But you know, I'm kind of old-fashioned. I never had any desire to just live with a guy. Moving in together ought to be a bigger commitment than sharing refrigerator and bathroom space."

He was silent for so long she wondered if this time she'd gone too far. She was searching frantically for something else to say when he relieved all her fears. "I am old-fashioned like that, too," he said. He cleared his throat. "Which is why I was hoping I could talk you into marrying me."

Her eyes widened and her mouth dropped open. "You…you mean that?" she asked.

"I meant what I said—you are the only woman I want to be with."

"Then yes. Yes, I'll marry you!" She threw her arms around him and kissed him soundly. "Yes, yes, yes!"

He had to pull the truck over to the side of the road to avoid running into a ditch, then he wrapped his arms around her and kissed her. *Yes, yes, yes!* continued to echo in her head. After so many nos—no, she couldn't race again; no, she'd never have an Olympic medal; no, she'd never be the best woman skier in the world—yes was one of the sweetest words she knew.

Past failures had hurt her, as they had hurt Hagan, but together they could heal. They could have love and they could have each other.

That was really all they needed.

Epilogue

For the second time this year, Hagan was wearing a tuxedo and standing in front of a preacher. Beside him, Max fidgeted and Hagan fought his own wave of nervousness. He felt in his pocket for the ring and took a deep breath. Nothing to worry about.

Heather completed her stately procession down the flagstone path between rows of chairs arranged at the Mountain Wedding Garden. The garden, located in a secluded glen near the town of Crested Butte, offered a postcard view of the surrounding mountains and fields of blooming wildflowers.

As Heather took her place across from Hagan, the organist pounded out the first chords of "The Wedding March." The guests shuffled to their feet and turned to watch Casey walk up the path on the arm of her father.

Hagan glanced at Max, who was smiling so broadly his face must have hurt, then turned and found Maddie in the crowd. She caught his eye and smiled also, a look that made his heart feel too large for his chest.

In a few more weeks, she would be the one walking down the aisle in a white dress, and he would be the man waiting for her. The day could not come soon enough for him.

Casey took her place next to Max, the preacher said a few words, then Zephyr came forward, carrying his guitar. A slight limp was the only reminder of the injuries he had suffered three months previously, and it obviously had not affected his singing, as he launched into a heartfelt love song.

When it was time for the vows, Hagan did his part and handed over the ring. The bride and groom kissed, their guests applauded and Hagan went in search of Maddie.

He found her near the entrance to the Town Park pavilion, where the reception was to be held. She was standing with Zephyr and Trish. "You did a very nice job on your song," Hagan told his friend.

"Thanks. I wrote it especially for this occasion."

"Then you've been busy," Maddie said. "Working for Max and I see Moose Juice has bookings all over town."

He grinned. "The best is yet to come. I've got big plans."

"He really does," Trish said, leaning against him, her arm around his waist. "He's amazing."

He kissed her cheek. "I have to go. Moose Juice is providing the music for the reception."

The bride and groom approached then, Casey looking radiant in her ruffle-trimmed gown. Max had already ditched his tie and cummerbund and was looking more like himself. "I wanted you to meet my parents," Casey said, indicating the older couple beside her. "Ada and Charles Jernigan, this is Hagan Ansdar, Maddie Alexander and Trish Sanders."

"I hope you're enjoying your visit to Crested Butte," Trish said.

"Yes. It's a lovely place." Ada smiled graciously. She was a polished, older version of her daughter, expensively groomed and wearing a diamond choker Hagan guessed was worth more than he made in a year. She was the kind of woman who would have stood out in any crowd, but especially here in this casual setting.

Max's parents joined them. His mother, Delia, put a hand on Hagan's arm. "Hello there," she said. "I don't know if you remember me. We met last summer."

"Of course I remember you." He put an arm around Maddie and drew her forward. "This is my fiancée, Maddie Alexander. Maddie, this is Max's mother, Delia Overbridge."

"Lucky you," Delia said, shaking Maddie's hand. "When is the wedding?"

"Next month." Maddie smiled up at Hagan. "Then we're honeymooning in Norway."

"Congratulations to you both." The band started and Delia turned to her husband. "Marvin, let's dance," she said.

"The newlyweds are supposed to dance first," Marvin protested.

"No, no, we don't want any of that," Max said. "You all have to dance with us."

Hagan turned to Maddie. "Shall we dance?"

She moved easily into his arms and looked up at him as Zephyr and his band played a slightly faster version of the love song he had performed for the wedding. "No one is staring at us this time," she said. "I guess we're old news."

"That is the way I like it." He guided her around the Overbridges, who were swaying together with more enthusiasm than skill, past Bryan and his new girlfriend Ilsa, who was apparently taking a dance lesson there on the floor. He looked across at Max and Casey, arm in arm and clearly oblivious to anyone else on the floor, focused only on each other.

He looked down at Maddie and thought again how lucky he was to have found her. His life had been so empty before, and he had not even known what was missing until she came along. "Do you believe in soul mates?" he asked. "That people exist who were meant to be together?"

She studied him, eyes shining, then nodded. "I think maybe I do. Do you?"

"I never did before," he said. "But I am beginning to change my mind." He tightened his hold on her. With Maddie, he could believe in all kinds of things. Maybe even in a love that lasted forever.

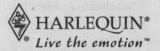

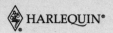

REQUEST YOUR FREE BOOKS!
2 FREE NOVELS PLUS 2
FREE GIFTS!

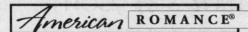 *American* **ROMANCE**®

Heart, Home & Happiness!

YES! Please send me 2 FREE Harlequin American Romance® novels and my 2 FREE gifts. After receiving them, if I don't wish to receive any more books, I can return the shipping statement marked "cancel." If I don't cancel, I will receive 4 brand-new novels every month and be billed just $4.24 per book in the U.S., or $4.99 per book in Canada, plus 25¢ shipping and handling per book and applicable taxes, if any*. That's a savings of close to 15% off the cover price! I understand that accepting the 2 free books and gifts places me under no obligation to buy anything. I can always return a shipment and cancel at any time. Even if I never buy another book from Harlequin, the two free books and gifts are mine to keep forever.

154 HDN EEZK   354 HDN EEZV

Name _____ (PLEASE PRINT) _____

Address _____ Apt. # _____

City _____ State/Prov. _____ Zip/Postal Code _____

Signature (if under 18, a parent or guardian must sign)

Mail to the **Harlequin Reader Service**®:
IN U.S.A.: P.O. Box 1867, Buffalo, NY 14240-1867
IN CANADA: P.O. Box 609, Fort Erie, Ontario L2A 5X3

Not valid to current Harlequin American Romance subscribers.

Want to try two free books from another line?
Call 1-800-873-8635 or visit www.morefreebooks.com.

* Terms and prices subject to change without notice. NY residents add applicable sales tax. Canadian residents will be charged applicable provincial taxes and GST. This offer is limited to one order per household. All orders subject to approval. Credit or debit balances in a customer's account(s) may be offset by any other outstanding balance owed by or to the customer. Please allow 4 to 6 weeks for delivery.

Your Privacy: Harlequin is committed to protecting your privacy. Our Privacy Policy is available online at www.eHarlequin.com or upon request from the Reader Service. From time to time we make our lists of customers available to reputable firms who may have a product or service of interest to you. If you would prefer we not share your name and address, please check here. ☐

HAR07